Snowfall

By Shelley Shepard Gray

Sisters of the Heart series
HIDDEN
WANTED
FORGIVEN
GRACE

Seasons of Sugarcreek series
WINTER'S AWAKENING
SPRING'S RENEWAL
AUTUMN'S PROMISE
CHRISTMAS IN SUGARCREEK

Families of Honor
THE CAREGIVER
THE PROTECTOR
THE SURVIVOR
A CHRISTMAS FOR KATIE (NOVELLA)

The Secrets of Crittenden County
MISSING
THE SEARCH
FOUND
PEACE

The Days of Redemption series
DAYBREAK
RAY OF LIGHT
EVENTIDE

Return to Sugarcreek series
HOPEFUL
THANKFUL
JOYFUL

Other books
REDEMPTION

Snowfall

A Days of Redemption Christmas Novella

SHELLEY SHEPARD GRAY

AVON

INSPIRE

An Imprint of HarperCollins*Publishers*

P.S.™ is a trademark of HarperCollins Publishers.

HarperCollins books may be purchased for educational, business, or sales promotional use. For information please e-mail the Special Markets Department at SPsales@harpercollins.com.

FIRST EDITION

Library of Congress Cataloging-in-Publication Data

Gray, Shelley Shepard.
    Snowfall : a days of redemption Christmas novella / Shelley Shepard Gray.
        pages cm.— (Days of redemption)
    Summary: *New York Times* bestselling author Shelley Shepard Gray spins a beautiful holiday tale of finding love in unexpected places.
    ISBN 978-0-06-220454-7 (paperback)
    1. Amish—Fiction. 2. Christmas stories. I. Title.
    PS3607.R3966S64 2014
    813'.6—dc23
                                                          2014015804

14 15 16 17 18 OV/RRD 10 9 8 7 6 5 4 3 2 1

To Lynne and Laurie, a terrific mother-daughter team who also would have known just what to do with six Rhodes kinner

It is more blessed to give than to receive.

Acts 20:35

Snowflakes are such fragile things, but look what happens when they stick together.

Amish proverb

Who made the snow waits where love is.

From the poem, "The Snow Is Deep on the Ground" by Kenneth Patchen

Chapter 1

Babysitters are supposed to like kinner. That's a rule, I think.

Thomas, Age 8

They were horrible children.

Well, perhaps that was an exaggeration. The *kinner* weren't horrible, exactly. They were simply too much for one sixty-three-year-old woman to handle for six hours at a time.

As Lovina Keim watched the chaos unfold around her in Martin Rhodes's kitchen, she wondered, yet again, how she had gotten herself into such a situation. She wasn't all that old—certainly not! But at this time in her life, she should be spending her free time working on a crossword puzzle or crocheting a blanket for a friend's adorable new baby girl. Or, perhaps even reading one of the novels in her To-Be-Read pile.

Instead, she was surrounded by no less than six unruly children and one rambunctious golden retriever puppy. Worst of all, not a one of them could mind manners or follow directions.

For sure and for certain, she had had enough. Furthermore, she'd had enough about two hours ago.

"Are you going to sit there forever, Miss Lovina?" Seven-year-old Gregory asked, placing sticky fingers on the back of her chair.

"Only as long as I have to," she replied.

Nine-year-old Katrina wrinkled her nose. "What does that mean?"

"It means I will be here only until my grandson Roman comes to pick me up in his buggy." Which, by the way, couldn't come soon enough.

"When's that?"

She darted a glance at the ridiculous wooden cuckoo clock hanging on the wall over the door. "In five minutes, if the Lord is *gut*."

"But what if He ain't *gut*?" Brigit asked from her other side. "What are ya gonna do then?" It had taken Lovina exactly five minutes to realize that Brigit and her twin, Karin, were impertinent.

"I suppose the Lord will let me know. But I don't imagine Roman will be late. He's a preacher, you know." And because she was so very proud of her grandson—and who wouldn't be?—she let her pride shine through. "Preachers are important people in our church community."

"Daed says preachers ain't any smarter than he is," Thomas said from his perch atop the kitchen counter. The very same kitchen counter that she'd wiped off four times but that was now covered in smudges of peanut butter. "He says they're just lucky."

"I don't believe in luck, and your father shouldn't, either," she replied sharply. But because she was a guest in their home—and because she liked the fact that he was four feet away from her—she refrained from ordering Thomas off the counter. At eight years of age, he was already showing signs that he would welcome a life in the circus. At this point, she was simply glad he was remaining in one spot.

"I'm gonna tell my father you said that," Thomas retorted.

"Me, too," Meg, the littlest Rhodes, said from her position on the floor. She'd decided to brush Frank, the nine-month-old puppy, on the kitchen floor. Currently, she was brushing the golden retriever with enough care to enter him into a dog show. She was also causing blond dog hair to fly everywhere.

When she'd first arrived, Lovina had attempted to sweep up the mess. But within seconds, she realized that her dark gray dress attracted the fur like a magnet. After that, she'd decided to stay as far away from both the puppy and the scattered wisps of fur as possible. With a weary sigh, she attempted to brush some of the fur off her gray dress. But it was a useless, counterproductive activity. The fur stubbornly remained fixed to the fabric.

Kind of like the peanut butter that had gotten smeared on her black bonnet.

Or the ink from the pen that had exploded when she'd tried to write their father a note.

She was going to need a good bath the moment she got away from this house. And some pain reliever, too.

Just as the clock struck four with a melodic chirp, the back door opened. Lovina jumped to her feet. "Roman, thank goodness you are back!"

"I'm afraid it's only me, Lovina," Martin, the *kinners'* father said apologetically. "I came to see how everyone is, uh, doing. . . ." His voice drifted off as he took in Thomas perched on the counter, Meg sitting on the floor with Frank, and the other four *kinner* scattered about the room. Even to Lovina's eyes they looked bored, unhappy, and restless.

Without a sound, his eyes darted to the dirty countertops, the sink filled with dishes, the hair on the floor. Finally, he settled his eyes on Lovina, sitting in the middle of it all.

He inhaled sharply, obviously holding back some harsh criticism.

Lovina supposed she couldn't blame him. She certainly never would have imagined that she could be bested by six small children. But in her defense, she'd never experienced any children like the ones surrounding her.

After taking a deep breath, Martin spoke. "What's going on, Lovina? I would have thought you would have things well in hand."

"I did." Well, she had for about five seconds.

"I thought you were going to make supper."

Lovina stood up, walked to the rickety coat rack near the back door, and pulled off her cloak. She slipped it over her shoulders and fastened the button at the collar. "I did make you supper," she snapped. "It is in the refrigerator. Simply heat it for thirty minutes when you are ready to eat."

He ran a hand over his face. "But what about everything else? You were going to clean up a bit."

She almost felt guilty when she spied the sink full of dirty dishes. But then, when she remembered just how much trouble the children could get into when her back was turned, every ounce of guilt floated away. "Cleaning was an impossibility," she muttered.

"Hmm." Looking at each of his children as if they were strangers, Martin added, "And I thought you were going to entertain them, too?"

Her chin lifted. "Martin, the last thing your *kinner* need is more entertainment."

He stared at her for a moment, then turned to the two boys and four girls who were slowly inching closer to him. "Children, what did you do to Miss Lovina?"

Katrina shrugged. "Nothing, Daddy."

"Are you sure?"

"Uh-huh. We were only being ourselves."

"But I asked you to be on your best behavior."

Thomas hopped off the countertop. "It weren't our fault that the pen exploded or that Frank knocked over Miss Lovina's *kaffi*. And it ain't my fault that the *kaffi* was really hot, either."

"Or that Meg threw up," Katrina said.

Martin was starting to look alarmed. "Meg threw up?"

"She is fine," Lovina said. "She simply ate too much candy."

"Candy?"

"She found the candy I had left over from the fall party," Karin whined. "Now there's none left."

"You shouldn't have kept any candy hidden in your room in an old shoebox," Katrina pointed out.

"You shouldn't have been snooping in our things with Meg. Nobody's allowed under our beds except Brigit and me," Karin retorted, looking, Lovina decided, far older than five years of age.

Her twin tugged on their father's pant leg. "Don't

worry, Daddy. Your chair isn't stained too bad. And Miss Lovina said in two years it might smell *gut* again."

Looking thunderous, Martin pointed to the doorway leading to the rest of the house. "*Kinner*, go to your rooms."

"Why?" Gregory asked. "We didn't do anything wrong."

"I'll tell you the why of it later. Now, go on."

"Can I take Frank with me?" Meg asked.

Lovina could answer that one. "Please. Do."

After darting several more looks their father's way, all six of the children trotted out of the kitchen, Frank scampering in the midst of them.

Once the room was cleared, Martin eased onto one of the chairs. "Lovina, what is going on? When Miss Freida, their regular sitter, told me you could help out around here until New Year's Day, I thought this had been your idea. I mean, you raised six *kinner* of your own, *jah*?"

"I did, indeed, raise six *kinner*. However, mine were far better behaved. I won't be returning."

"But they are out of school until the sixth of January and it's only December fifteenth."

"Martin, I am sorry, but for the life of me I canna think of one good reason to subject myself to three more weeks of being here. I'm old but not an idiot."

"But it's almost Christmas and Freida is on vacation. You must realize that I own a Christmas tree farm. This is my busiest time of the year."

"I am sorry about that. I, um, will try to find someone to take my place," she added before she could think better of it. "There must be someone who would be willing to put up with your *kinner* for twenty more days."

Martin was prevented from replying when a knock sounded at the door.

Hoping and praying it was her grandson, Lovina strode to the door and opened it in an instant. As soon as she spied her handsome grandson, she breathed easy for the first time all day. "Roman, aren't you a sight for sore eyes."

After hugging his grandmother, Roman turned to Martin. "*Gut* to see you, Martin. How goes it?"

"Not so well at the moment."

"Oh?"

Lovina linked her arm through her grandson's. "I'll tell you all about it when we get on our way, dear. It is time to go. Past time."

Roman's eyes narrowed as he gazed at her, then clapped Martin on the shoulder. "I think it might be best if I went on my way. But, listen, I'll come by soon and visit with ya. When we all have more time."

"Sure. That will be *gut*."

Now that she was about to leave the house, she

was feeling a bit guilty. Martin Rhodes really did have his hands full. "I really will try to find you a replacement, Martin," she said, suddenly thinking of a certain blue-eyed girl who'd just been let go from her job at Daybreak Retirement Home due to some recent budget cuts. The last time Lovina had volunteered there, one of the residents had whispered that he was worried about the young woman. Ruth had been a favorite of everyone's, and people were concerned that she was losing her income so close to Christmas.

"I would appreciate any help you could offer," Martin said.

Lovina nodded before following her grandson out the door. She turned around quickly and said, "In the meantime, I hope you will enjoy the casserole."

For the first time since he'd walked in the door, a spark of interest lit his eyes. "Ah, yes. It will be a treat to have a homemade dish. What kind is it?"

"Liver and onions."

She was so pleased to be walking out the door she almost didn't feel remorseful about the look of dismay on Martin's face.

She had freedom at last! It had never felt so sweet.

Chapter 2

Our mamm was real pretty. She used to laugh and tease Daed when he grumbled. Her name was Mamm.

Katrina, Age 9

The moment the Keims' black buggy rolled away, Martin breathed a sigh of relief. He respected Lovina Keim, he truly did. Pretty much everyone in Berlin respected the matriarch of the Keim family.

But he also found her exhausting.

Which was really too bad, because he'd been hoping that she would be the answer to his prayers. When Freida had asked for a whole month of vacation, he hadn't had the heart to refuse her request. Freida did so much for all of them.

Lovina stepping in had solved everything. But instead of restoring order in his house and comforting his children, the formidable lady had managed to allow even more chaos.

He honestly hadn't thought that could be possible.

Every night when he went to sleep, Martin asked God why He'd chosen him to carry so many burdens. There had to be a reason he was a widower raising six children all alone. Had to be.

It wasn't that he was resentful. *Nee*, far from that. The truth of the matter was that he didn't really mind having a lot of responsibility. And though he still mourned the loss of his sweet wife, Grace, Martin had come to terms with her death. It was no one's fault that she had a weak heart that had been further weakened by six pregnancies.

No one had known about that—well, no one but the Lord.

If Martin had known about her heart, he would have made sure to get her to the best doctors, made sure she received the best treatment possible.

But Grace hadn't been the type of woman to complain, and he hadn't been the type of man to question when she hadn't looked quite like herself. Now he had to live with the guilt and the knowledge that if he had been a little bit more concerned about Grace's health instead of merely trying to keep the farm afloat, his wife might still be by his side.

And now his problems seemed to keep snowballing. These days there were many moments when he ached to simply sit down, close his eyes, and let the rest of the world continue on without him.

Here it was, less than two weeks until Christmas. His busiest time of the year at their Christmas-tree farm, and he had no idea how he was going to care for his children. To make matters worse, he needed to keep focused on work. Last year business had been especially slow and they hadn't made anywhere near the profit they usually did. Consequently, he'd had to take out a loan to help pay his bills. Now he owed money to the bank and to his partner, Floyd. If he couldn't pay it back soon he might even lose the house. He might even lose the farm.

He had to make things right. But he couldn't do that if he had to stay home with the *kinner*.

Walking to the kitchen sink, he turned on the faucet and squirted a generous amount of dish soap onto the stack of dishes. As soapy water filled the sink, he found his mind drifting to better times.

Back when he was seventeen, Martin had finally taken matters into his own hands and moved to Ohio. He'd grown up just outside Shipshewana with his three brothers and two sisters, in a family that was far from perfect. His parents were two people who were perfectly nice on their own. But together? It was as if someone had lit a fuse between them. His earliest memory was listening to them argue and fight.

When he'd met Grace at a singing one Sunday

evening when he was sixteen, he'd been sure she was the woman for him. It had been she who'd encouraged him to leave Indiana and move to Ohio, cautioning him that everyone had to find their happiness one way or another.

So they'd moved, against his parents' wishes, against her parents' advice. Against his siblings' warnings that he was making a mighty big mistake.

But Grace had held his hand and gazed up at him with sweet, shining eyes full of trust. And with that trust, he'd imagined anything was possible.

And for a while, everything had gone smoothly. He and Grace had worked hard. He'd made a fast friend out of Floyd Miller, and ten years ago, the two of them had bought the Christmas-tree farm, which had been on its last leg.

In no time at all, he and Floyd had been growing trees and marketing the farm. They'd turned a profit the first year. With the profits, they'd invested in the farm, each fixed up his home a bit, and they had planned for the future.

But then everything had changed two years ago, when his precious Grace died. While he tried to deal with his grief and his children's, the farm went into a slump. He was still trying to pull everyone out.

This year was supposed to be better. But here it was, less than two weeks until Christmas, and there was no snow. No snow for sleigh rides. No snow for the farm's almost-famous sledding hill. No snow for the Englischer tourists who loved to come to Amish country to tromp through the Snowfall Christmas Tree Farm, pay for sleigh rides, pay for sledding hills, pay for photographs in the winter wonderland.

For the last two weeks, all they'd had was bitter cold and brown, desolate-looking fields. And hardly a tourist in sight.

"Daed? Da-ed!"

"Huh?" With a start, Martin realized he'd been staring blankly out the window over the sink, his hands submerged in the hot, soapy water, for several minutes. And while he'd been doing that, all the *kinner* had snuck back downstairs.

They were currently standing in the kitchen. Looking hesitant and worried. Nervous.

He hated that. He pulled out a mixing bowl, rinsed it carefully, then started drying it. "What is it, Thomas?"

"Is Miss Lovina comin' back tomorrow?" Thomas somehow managed to curl his lip, as if his tone of voice wasn't displaying his displeasure enough.

"It doesn't look like it."

"*Gut.* I didn't like her."

"Son, that ain't no way to talk about your elders. You should be respectful."

"I thought it wasn't disrespectful if you were

tellin' the truth. And you like us telling the truth, right, Daed?"

"*Jah*. Yes, of course. But still . . ."

"Besides, I don't think she liked us, neither," one of the twins said as she stepped a little closer to one of Martin's legs as he set the bowl on the countertop, then picked up a measuring cup. "Every time she looked at us, she frowned. And she frowned a lot, Daddy."

Martin secretly thought Karin might be right. Lovina had looked at Roman like he was helping her escape a terrible, dark place.

And while he knew his *kinner* were challenging, they certainly weren't terrible. "Each of you grab a towel and help me dry these dishes."

To his amazement, each of his children, even Meg, went to one of the drawers and grabbed a towel. Then, for the next ten minutes, he washed and rinsed, and the *kinner* dried dishes.

When that was done, Martin opened the door to the refrigerator, pulled out the covered container, and set it out on the counter. "At least she cooked supper," he pointed out. "So, who is up for some liver and onions?" He was particularly proud of himself for sounding rather upbeat about the dish.

"Not me," said Katrina.

"Me, neither," Thomas said after Martin pulled off the foil covering. "It looks like dog food."

"Thomas, it doesn't look like dog food." At least, not exactly. And well, not even Frank was sniffing it, and he ate everything, even candles.

Feeling a tug on his shirt, he discovered his youngest was looking up at him with wide eyes. "Are you gonna eat it, Daed?"

Meg looked so frightened about the idea that he had to laugh. "*Nee,*" he declared as he picked her up and pressed his lips to her temple. "I don't care for liver and onions. Or dog food."

"What are we going to eat for supper then?" Karin, their resident worrier, asked.

"How does scrambled eggs, bacon, and toast sound?"

"Daed, we had that last night," his eldest pointed out.

"You don't have to eat eggs and bacon if you'd rather not, Katrina," he said patiently. "In fact, you may have as much liver-and-onion casserole as you would like."

When the *kinner* started laughing, he did, too. When it came to choosing between laughter and tears, he now chose the former. The good Lord knew he'd certainly cried his fair share of tears.

More than enough.

Chapter 3

*I want a kitten for Christmas. I think Frank
does, too.*

Meg, Age 4

Day 3 of Christmas Break

Martin had become a master at sipping coffee and
pretending that he hadn't a care on his mind. But if
there was ever a time when he found it rather difficult, it was this morning.

And that was because they were currently waiting
for one Ruth Stutzman. He knew next to nothing
about her. They belonged to different church dis-
tricts, and he couldn't remember ever meeting her
in town, either.

Though that shouldn't have been a great surprise.
He didn't ever notice women, even women who

his friends slyly mentioned were giving him special smiles or were going out of their way to chat with him. As far as he was concerned, his heart belonged to Grace and it always would.

After walking to the stove and warming up his cup, Martin realized that he didn't know much about Ruth Stutzman at all. Only that she was an acquaintance of Lovina Keim's, that she'd recently lost her job at the retirement home, and that she had agreed to help him care for his children during Christmas break.

Everything about the situation grated on him. He didn't like that Lovina Keim had told Ruth all about him. And all about his motherless *kinner.* And how he couldn't cook and how he was in dire need of a helping hand. Or several helping hands.

He'd been so appalled, he'd almost told Lovina that he didn't need her help to find a nanny.

But because he did, and because he had no idea how to contact this Ruth and had no other option for the children other than packing them up and taking them to work at the Christmas-tree farm, he'd instead conveyed his thanks.

But that didn't mean he liked being known as a helpless widower, or that he appreciated that folks at the Daybreak Retirement Home were talking about him.

It hurt a man's pride to be thought of as a charity case.

It almost physically hurt to realize that he was going to have to accept this Ruth Stutzman's help no matter what. He was that desperate. The trees weren't going to get chopped, transported, and sold by themselves. It was his job, which was why he'd said yes to Ruth, though just imagining what Ruth would be like made him cringe.

Already he was imagining an older woman with a bossy nature. After all, who else but a woman like that would be friends with Lovina Keim?

No doubt she would barely tolerate his brood, frown a lot, speak her mind even when no one asked for her opinion, and concentrate on keeping order in his home.

If they were lucky.

And though he would never allow a woman into his home who would be mean to his *kinner*, he was enough of a realist to realize that taking care of six *kinner* like his was enough to make even the kindest and most patient of women become a bit shrewish. Even his lovely Grace had lost her patience a time or two over the course of a day.

It was likely their temporary babysitter would lose patience, too.

And because of that, Martin knew his children would be sad and miserable. And, perhaps, a touch resentful that while their many friends were out playing, baking cookies, and doing whatever else small children liked to do over Christmas vacation, they were having to spend their days in the company of a grumpy old woman named Ruth.

Now, after working all day at the Christmas-tree farm, he was going to have to return each day, prepared to cajole his children to try to deal with Ruth just a little bit longer.

"Daed, do you see her?" Thomas asked from the doorway leading into the dining room that they never used anymore.

"Not yet."

"Is she late?"

Thomas was a busy, buzzing child. As restless as a beaver on holiday and twice as inquisitive. "*Nee*, son. She ain't late yet."

"Then why are you staring out the window and frowning?"

"I'm simply looking out the window and thinking. There's a difference."

"Ah." Pulling over a chair, Thomas settled by his side and mimicked his pose. "What are you thinking about?"

"This and that."

"Are you thinking about Christmas?" His question had just the right amount of hope in it to make Martin's lips curve up.

"I'm thinking about Christmas trees."

Thomas sighed. "That's all you think about."

"That is not true. I think about lots of other things, too."

"But mainly you think about trees."

Not in any hurry to share just how much he worried about Thomas and his siblings, Martin lifted his chin. "Son, those trees occupy a good portion of my mind these days for a *gut* reason. They're important to our livelihood. We need to sell lots of trees this year."

"Oh? Do ya think, maybe, we could have a tree in our house?"

At least one of the children asked this every year. "Nope."

"Even if it was a small, ugly one that nobody else wanted?"

"Not even then."

Thomas swung his feet. Shifted. Stood up and pressed his nose to the cold windowpane. After staring out the window thirty seconds, it was obvious he was bored. "Can I come with you today?"

"Nope."

"Why not?"

"Because we're cutting and loading trees today, son."

"I could help."

"I'm afraid you can't. It's dangerous work. I don't want you to get hurt."

He straightened his narrow shoulders. "I'm pretty strong."

It took everything Martin had to keep a serious expression. "You are a mighty fine boy. And you are strong for being only eight. But I'm afraid you're not big enough to help. Not yet. One day you will, though."

"When? Next year?"

"I'm thinking when you're twelve."

Thomas's eyes widened, then settled into his scowl. "That's forever from now."

"You should enjoy being eight, *boo*."

"I'm sick of staying home with old ladies."

Resting his hand on his boy's shoulders, Martin added, "I know it's hard, but someone needs to look after you all."

"It's boring. All Mrs. Keim wanted to do was sit in the kitchen and watch the clock."

Martin figured it would be best to say nothing about that. "Regardless, I have a feeling someday you'll be working so hard you'll be wishing for days like this."

"Days when I'm waiting for another grumpy babysitter? I don't think so."

"We don't know for sure if this one will be grumpy."

"Daed, she works with old people all day," Thomas

said with the supreme confidence that only a child could have. "She's gonna be grumpy."

Since Martin felt his son had a point, he pressed his lips together and started simply hoping for a reprieve from the questions.

It was almost a relief to see the horse and buggy clip-clopping up the driveway. "We shall soon find out, won't we?" Turning, he saw that his Katrina had the rest of the *kinner* lined up in the other room. They were standing in front of the window and looking out with various expressions of forbearance and dismay.

He stood up and carefully tucked his chair back under the kitchen table and motioned for Thomas to do the same. Then he stepped into the dining room and quietly spoke. "You all stay here while I go out and greet Ruth."

"Can you make sure she's nice, Daed?" Meg asked, her eyes filled with hope.

Reaching out, he pressed his hand on the top of his youngest child's *kapp*. "I will do my best," he promised.

While the children watched, Martin slipped on his coat, positioned his black stocking cap on his head, and then walked out the door just as the buggy came to a stop in front of one of the hitching posts in front of the house. Hoping all the while that this Ruth was going to be nicer than expected.

"Please, Lord," he quietly prayed. "Please, since it's almost Christmas and all, won't You consider giving me just a little bit of a break? 'Cause I could surely use some help here. Make this woman not be too terrible. My *kinner* have already lost their mother. They don't need a sourpuss babysitter, too."

As the cold wind brushed against his cheeks, he lifted his eyes to the heavens and gave a fierce look. Then, as Ruth's horse pawed restlessly at the dry, hard ground, he hurried over to help. "Hello," he called out, just as Ruth Stutzman deftly hopped out of the buggy. Their eyes met. After the briefest of pauses, she smiled.

Martin blinked. And then, to his embarrassment, he blinked again, just as if he'd never seen a woman before.

Ruth Stutzman was young. And pretty, too. She had dark, wavy hair and bright blue eyes. A smattering of freckles danced across her nose, and the palest of pink brightened her cheeks. She was of medium height and blessed with the kind of curves he'd always thought women should have but always tried hard to not think about.

Maybe it was because she'd taken him so off-guard, or maybe because he was sadly out of practice when it came to conversing with pretty women, but he blurted the first thing that came to mind. "You are nothing like I expected."

Raising a pair of finely arched eyebrows, her smile turned into a full-fledged grin. "Isn't that something? I was just thinking the same thing about you."

Martin wasn't sure if that was a compliment or not. And because he was so confused about his reaction, he turned away and grabbed hold of the horse. "It's too cold for your horse to be out here for long. I'll take him into the barn."

"I've got a blanket for him in the back of the buggy. Would you like me to cover him for you?"

"*Nee.*"

She stared at him, obviously waiting for him to explain himself, or say that he would take care of the blanket.

But he did neither. He simply stood still, holding the gelding's reins. He had never been a man of many words.

But suddenly, well, absolutely not a single one came to mind. Not a single, solitary one.

As Ruth gazed at Martin Rhodes, she reflected that there had to be a first time for everything.

And at the moment, she was standing in front of a man who seemed to be tongue-tied. Furthermore, all she seemed to be able to do was smile.

Fact was, Martin Rhodes was brawny and tall, with lightly tanned skin, green eyes, and thick, dark brown hair. He was much more handsome than any father of six children had the right to be.

In short, he was nothing like she'd imagined, and she'd spent quite a bit of time last night wondering what he would be like.

Ruth wasn't so sure how she felt about that.

Though he was now holding her gelding's reins, he was facing her again. As she felt his eyes skim over her from head to toe, she stood still and gazed unabashedly at him. She knew she wasn't the prettiest girl in the world. Far from that. Her measurements were a little too big, her features a little too bold.

After another few seconds stretched between them, he blurted, "What did you think I was going to be like?"

She had a lot of answers to that one. None of which seemed appropriate. So she cut to the chase and said the first thing that popped into her head, "Older."

He laughed. "I thought the same thing about you." As her horse nudged him with his nose, Martin rubbed his muzzle. "Looks like you've got a fairly forthright horse here."

"His name is Rocky. He's my landlady's horse, but I have found him to be a bit forthright as well."

"Perhaps it's a good match."

"Maybe so. I've grown to be very fond of him."

"I'll go put him in a stall. Would you like to go

with me to the barn? Or would you rather go on inside and meet my *kinner*?"

"Which would you prefer?"

"Well, if you walk with me, you'll get a moment's reprieve from my children." He nodded toward the house. "They're waiting for you, you see."

She turned her head and saw six small faces staring back at her. Two boys, four girls. Not a one of the children was smiling.

But none of them was glaring, either.

Dear Lord, she silently prayed. *Remember my prayers*.

Martin was staring at her, too. "Do you like children?"

"I think so."

"You think so? Don't you know?"

"Well, I don't know these *kinner*, so I don't know if I'll like them," she teased.

But instead of being amused, he looked like he was tempted to roll his eyes. "I meant, do you like spending time with *kinner*? Do you enjoy watching them?"

She opted for the truth. "I don't know. I don't have much experience watching children."

"Then why did you want to come here?"

"I didn't. I somehow got talked into it by Lovina Keim. And then, well, I just got laid off from my job at Daybreak." When she noticed his eyes turn sympathetic, she explained. "Budget cuts."

"That's hard. I'm sorry about that."

"I am, too. However I am grateful for this opportunity." And suddenly, she realized she *was* glad. Not only had she been worried about her finances, she'd also been dreading the thought of spending another Christmas season alone. After her parents died when she was only five, Ruth had become her extended family's charity case. They'd all taken her in for a year at a time, sometimes grudgingly, sometimes with kind hearts. But no matter what the situation, Ruth had learned over time that she was never to get too attached. That it could only bring more heartbreak.

Now, at the very least, Martin was going to pay her, and she would be surrounded by noise and chatter. Even if the *kinner* were as rambunctious as Lovina had described, Ruth knew it would be far more difficult to be sitting in her rented room completely alone.

Green eyes danced. "Just to let you know, Lovina talked circles around me, too." Patting the horse again, he added, "She's the kind of woman who makes me glad I spend most of my time with trees and horses."

Surprising herself, Ruth chuckled.

His smile grew brighter. "So, Ruth, would you like to walk to the barn with me . . . or are you ready to go in and meet the children?"

Maybe it was because he was still absently patting

Rocky. Maybe it was because he looked just as apprehensive as she felt. Or maybe it was because she'd spied something in his children's faces that looked a whole lot like optimism.

Whatever the reason, she quickly reached into the buggy's interior and pulled out a large picnic hamper. "I think I'll go on in and meet your children. They've been awfully patient."

"Might be a good idea. They've been alone for ten minutes."

"They're that rambunctious?"

His lips twitched. "They are. Hey, what's in the hamper?"

"A surprise for the *kinner*."

He stared at it as if he was afraid it was about to explode. "There's no handcuffs inside, is there?"

"Not today, Martin." She shrugged, enjoying the silly, irreverent conversation. "But if they misbehave, I might have to resort to such tricks tomorrow," she joked.

Martin looked at her with eyes wide. "Ruth, you just made me the happiest man on earth."

"And why is that?"

"Because you're already talking about coming back." He chuckled. "All right, well, then, once I get Rocky settled, I'll head off to the farm. But don't worry, I'll come in first to make sure you are all set."

"That won't be necessary." Making a shooing gesture with her hands, she said, "Go on now, we'll be fine."

"Are you sure?"

"Very much so."

"All right. I'll return in three hours."

"Wait—is there anything I need to know?"

"Yeah. There's six of 'em. Make sure when I come back that's still the case."

Unable to help herself, she laughed. Maybe being here wasn't going to be so bad after all. Maybe, just maybe.

Chapter 4

*I talk more than Karin. That's how you can tell
us apart. Plus I've got a freckle on my left pinky.*

Brigit, Age 5

Still feeling hopeful after her promising conversation
with Martin, Ruth picked up her wicker hamper and
trotted into his home. Maybe this wouldn't be such
a difficult job, after all.

Perhaps the kids would be just as appreciative and
kind as their father. Maybe they wouldn't realize she
had little experience with people their age, or they
wouldn't hold it against her.

Perhaps she would actually like being with them, and
they would like being with her. It might even be fun
teaching the children to make some Christmas crafts.

Plus, she could be around all of them during the
Christmas holidays. And wouldn't that be some-

thing? Though she enjoyed her days at the retirement home a lot, being with a family was exciting. It had been a long time since she had felt included, really included. She hadn't been in an actual home in more than a year. She hadn't been in a home where she'd been happy for longer than she cared to remember.

Especially since she always tried her best not to remember.

The Rhodeses' door needed a fresh coat of paint. Okay, it needed more than that. It needed to be sanded and painted a bright, glossy black. Currently it looked as if it had once been stained brown or maybe gray. It looked dark and dismal against the house's white siding. The whole outside of the house would look much better if a coat or two of paint were applied.

If the weather warmed a bit, perhaps the children could help her paint the door. They could sand the wood and then carefully paint the door black and the trim around it a fresh, bright white. She seemed to remember hearing that children liked projects.

Now filled to the brim with good intentions, she turned the handle and walked through a small mudroom into a spacious kitchen. At first glance, it looked just as neglected as that front door. Though everything looked clean enough, there was a tired air about it that made her think no one had given it anything but minimal attention for a quite a while.

Just as she set her basket on the center of the kitchen table, a line of children entered the room. They were beautiful *kinner*, four blessed with dark brown hair and green eyes, two with blond hair and brown eyes.

Every one of them was watching her intently. Not a one was smiling. Instead, they were looking at her the way she might look at a stray cat in her yard. She wouldn't be mean to it, but she wouldn't especially want a strange animal living in her midst, either.

And in that instant, all her optimism fled as reality set in. This wasn't going to be all that different from her life with all of those distant relatives.

"Hi," she said. "I'm Ruth." When no one replied, she cleared her throat. "I'm going to be looking after you until New Year's Day. I expect your father already told you this."

When they continued to eye her silently, she started to think that this Christmas could be even worse than the ones she'd known. Feeling dismayed, she attempted to joke. "I know this is hard, having a new sitter and all. But I'd like to make the best of things. I'd like to get to know you, and I'm hoping that you all can tell me how to do things. I'm going to need a lot of help, you see."

Finally, finally, the oldest girl spoke. "Why are you going to be needin' our help?"

Ruth blinked. She hadn't planned to tell them

much about her personal life. She'd hoped to come across as confident and self-assured.

But as she stared into the clear, wary eyes of the little girl, Ruth knew she had no desire to try to pull anything over on them. It was obvious that these *kinner* were expecting the worst—and that they could probably spy a liar from fifty feet away.

Therefore, she decided honesty was the best policy. "I'm going to be needin' your help because I don't have much experience with children."

"Why not?" one of the boys asked.

There was no way she was going to start telling them the specifics about her life. "Just because I don't."

"But what about your brothers or sisters?" another girl asked. She was one of the twins. Her voice was a little less accusatory, a little more confused.

Ruth crossed her arms over her chest and contemplated just how much she wanted to share. Not much. On the other hand, it didn't look as if these *kinner* were going to give her much of an option.

Bracing herself, she replied—and prepared to answer an onslaught of questions. "I don't have any brothers or sisters."

The eldest girl tilted her head to one side. "You are an only child?"

"I am."

"What about your cousins?"

"I'm afraid I'm not too close to my cousins. I don't

see them often." Actually, she hadn't seen them since she'd left their house after her year with them.

"Well, who do you have?" one of the twins asked. "Everyone has family."

"That is not for you to find out," she said smartly.

In response, the line of *kinner* blinked and then blinked again. Good, she had gotten them a little off-kilter.

Perhaps this was the tack she should adopt. Stay on the offensive.

"Now, please introduce yourselves and tell me your age and one thing you'd like to do with me while I'm here."

"Do?" a boy interrupted.

"*Jah*. I'm talking about activities. You all need to tell me what projects you'd like to do with me over Christmas break. After that, we'll figure out what you want to do first."

The children looked at one another in confusion, as if she'd suddenly decided they should take a trip to the moon. Then, after a bit of a hesitation, the eldest girl stepped forward. "I'm Katrina, I'm nine, and I don't know what I want to do with you."

Ruth nodded sagely. "I suppose that makes sense. After all, we don't know each other, do we?"

Katrina shook her head slowly. Every inch of her seemed to scream that she was communicating with Ruth reluctantly, almost in spite of herself.

Clearing her throat, Ruth propped her hands on her hips. "Next?"

The twin girls stepped forward together. "I'm Brigit and this is Karin," the bossy one said. "We're five and we're twins."

"Ah."

"Like she couldn't figure that out," one of the boys scoffed. "You both look just alike, and you always dress alike, too."

Ruth ignored that. "Brigit, what would you like to do with me?"

"I don't know."

"Karin?" Ruth said gently. "Do you like to bake cookies or go for walks?"

Karin looked at the oven, the door, and then at her sister. And then, ever so slowly, she shook her head. "*Nee.*"

"I'm sorry to hear you say that. I love to bake cookies and I always need help."

Little Karin's eyes turned to saucers but she stayed silent.

Ruth had imagined that they might not like a stranger caring for them, but she didn't understand why they were being so standoffish. Why were they so reluctant to reach out to her?

Feeling more and more dismayed, Ruth made a shooing motion with her hand. "All right, boys, it's your turn. What are your names?"

The smaller of the two stepped forward. "I'm Gregory and I'm seven. And I hope you don't stay long."

"And why is that?"

"You don't seem nice."

These had to be some of the rudest children in the state of Ohio! "At the moment, you don't seem too nice, either."

That earned her her first smile—from the oldest boy. He had curly light brown hair and what she was already suspecting to be a deceptively angelic expression. "You're funny, Ruth."

"I'm blunt, that's what I am. What is your name and age?"

"Thomas. I'm eight. But everyone says I'm going on eighteen."

"Why is that?"

" 'Cause Thomas always wants to be older," Katrina supplied.

"Now, that is mighty interesting." Actually, she thought it was amusing, but she didn't want to hurt his feelings.

"Why? Do you want to be older, too?"

"Definitely not." She had a lot to accomplish before she got much older!

"How come? How old are you?"

"My age is none of your business." She neatly cut him off before he could argue with that. "Now, what would you like to do with me?"

"That is none of your business." He smiled again, somewhat evilly.

But then he marched over to the smallest member of the family, a little girl who was holding a worn white blanket that looked to be in dire need of a wash. "Go ahead, Meg," he murmured, his voice soft and gentle. "She won't care what you say."

But instead of saying a word, the littlest girl popped her thumb in her mouth and leaned in to Thomas.

Rolling his eyes, he nonetheless wrapped one arm around his sister. "This here is Meg. She's four and shy. She doesn't want to do anything with you, either."

Feeling stunned, hurt, and a bit mystified by the children's obvious plan to keep her at arm's length, she sighed.

It looked like some things never changed.

Old feelings, carefully shuttered, threatened to burst open and take control. Once again, she was the new girl in a distant relative's house. Standing in a kitchen, all of her belongings in the world folded carefully in an old duffle bag. Relying on the kindness of others and—in spite of knowing better—daring to hope that things were going to improve.

For a moment, she was tempted to turn right around and march out to the barn. To hitch up Rocky, locate Martin, and inform him that she was sorry but that she had no desire to spend the next few weeks with his *kinner*. She'd already come too far in her life to once again be at the mercy of six children with a bone to pick with the world.

She'd been there and done that.

But then she noticed how Thomas was still holding his sister Meg protectively, as if he was used to shielding her from the world. As if he was used to giving her that little bit of warmth and attention that she needed. Like he knew all about being considered a burden.

When she met his eyes, his gaze was stern and solemn and vaguely taunting. As if he was prepared to protect little Meg no matter what.

And that, of course, made her heart melt. And suddenly, it all made sense.

At least, it did to her.

She had plenty of experience wishing that someone would take the time to shield her from the harsh realities of life. Boy, how many days had she spent as a little girl wishing for someone—anyone—to offer her a warm hug? A kind smile? She would have hardly known what to do if someone had carefully placed a comforting arm around her.

These children were somehow conditioned to not expect too much. Furthermore, it looked as if they'd taken to shielding themselves against further pain and disappointment.

She, too, had done that a time or two.

Instinctively, she knew that they wouldn't respond to anything fake—or anything that bordered on too intrusive in their lives. If they saw her as desperate or insincere, they would run, run away as fast as they could!

"Well, Katrina, Thomas, Gregory, Brigit, Karin, and Meg, I am sorry none of you want to do anything special with me today. But that is okay. I'm glad you were honest."

Gregory wrinkled his nose. "You are?"

"Oh, for sure and for certain! You are children, not workers. If you don't wish to do any projects or activities with me, you certainly don't have to. I'll simply keep everything I brought in this hamper for safekeeping. Maybe the next group of children I'm around will be interested in it."

And just as she predicted—well, hoped—all six children's eyes fixated on her bright red wicker hamper.

Karin stepped forward. "You brought something for us?"

"I did. Well, I'd hoped to bring something for us to do. I like to be busy, you see. But I don't want to force you to do anything with me."

"You didn't force us. You asked us," Thomas stated. "Before you went and told us that there was something in that hamper for us."

Summoning up her best Lovina Keim impression, Ruth tipped her chin up a bit and attempted to look put upon. She had no idea how she was supposed to act with the children so she relied on what her instincts told her to do, and that was to play hard to get. "I doubt that would have made a difference, anyway. You six look like a pretty tough bunch."

Out of the corner of her eye, Ruth spied Katrina biting her lip. "We do?"

"You do to me." She brushed her hands together. "I understand I am supposed to cook you supper and clean your house as well. So that is what I suppose I should do." Waving a hand in her direction, she murmured, "Well, carry on, then."

Six little faces stared at her incredulously. "That's it?" Thomas asked. "You're just going to ignore us?"

"I'm not ignoring ya. I'm following your wishes. I'm not going to force myself—or my activities—on you if you are not interested. That isna right." She waved her hand. "Go on now. I'll simply go about my business. When I'm ready to see your bedrooms I'll find them myself."

A line formed between Thomas's eyebrows. "But what were you going to do if we wanted to see what was inside your hamper?"

"I was going to play games, of course."

"But what about all the cleaning you've got to do?"

"I don't know about you all, but I'd always rather

play a game than clean. But that's all right," she said as she rolled up her sleeves. "I am getting paid to do the best I can with what I'm given. That's all one can do, I suppose."

Quickly, she turned around because she was afraid she wouldn't be able to hide her smile any longer. Truly, the six of them looked like a pack of beagles eagerly anticipating a morning's hunt.

She heard some whispering behind her, but she pretended not to hear. Instead she resolutely turned on the faucet and squeezed a little bit of the dish soap in the sink.

"Ruth, wait!" Gregory exclaimed.

She turned off the water. "*Jah*, Gregory?"

"I want to see what is in the hamper."

"Me, too," little Meg said with a pleading look.

"I want to see, too!" Karin said. "And I didn't really mean that I didn't want to do anything with you. I was just trying to be diff'cult."

"Me, too," her twin said, just as a very furry golden retriever came in. And so does Frank."

"Frank?"

"He's our dog. He's a *gut* dog, too. But he chews."

"How about this. Tomorrow, if your father wants me to return, I'll bring my hamper back. We'll chat, and if you are in the mood to play games, we'll look inside."

"You can still change your mind today," Thomas reminded her. "It's not too late."

And at that, little Meg popped her thumb out of her mouth. "I want to make cookies with you, Ruth. Can I?"

"Of course. Go find a step stool, child. I would like your company. I would like it *verra* much."

Meg scampered to the other side of the kitchen, picked up the little step stool, and then proceeded to half carry, half drag the step stool to Ruth's side. When Ruth smiled at her again, she clambered on top of it and leaned close. "I like baking," she whispered.

"I do too, child," Ruth replied as she pulled a large ceramic bowl closer.

"What kind of cookies are you gonna make?" Meg asked.

"Peanut butter with chocolate kisses in the middle."

"But I don't think we have any of those chocolates."

"I brought some," Ruth said as she located the flour, sugar, peanut butter, and margarine. After measuring out the ingredients, she added two eggs and a dash of vanilla.

"Oh."

Five minutes later, the twins stopped lurking around the corner and asked if they could help roll cookies in sugar.

"Of course, girls. Get out some saucers so I can pour sugar into them."

She knew he was right. Ruth also knew that w\
was in her basket wasn't all that exciting. The ch\
dren looked like they were expecting her to pull o\
a menagerie of baby animals or the like.

So she decided to keep them waiting. Maybe they
would be a little bit more eager to talk to her. And,
well, her life had shown her time and again that
nothing easily gained was worth having.

She sighed. "Ach, but I'm afraid it is, Thomas.
Tomorrow is soon enough. Now I'm going to make
cookies on my own and a taco casserole."

Frank walked up to her and sat down by her feet.
When she glanced down at him, his tongue lolled
out and he gave her a tail thump. She bent down and
gave him a pat. "Oh, and it looks like I'll be keeping
company with your sweet dog, too. He seems to like
me fine."

Katrina folded her arms over her chest. "You
know, we could probably sneak a peek in the hamper
without you ever knowing."

"Maybe you could, and maybe you would do it,
too." She leaned down a bit, daring to look the nine-
year-old in the eye. "But if you did, you'd know that
you spoiled the surprise."

Wariness lit Katrina's eyes. "And?"

"And you might even come to regret that decision.
Sometimes it's better to try to get along with people,
yes? Wait until tomorrow, Katrina. I'll be back."

They did as she asked, then followed her movements, making lopsided balls out of the dough, then rolling each in lots of granulated sugar.

Then, in came Gregory, who asked to help put them on the baking sheet. Soon, Thomas and Katrina pulled up chairs, saying they were supposed to watch their siblings.

Every two minutes or so, Ruth would catch one of them eyeing the hamper with something akin to awe in their eyes.

All of them leaned close when she carefully pulled the bag of chocolate from the top of the hamper.

And by the time she'd served each of them no less than three cookies and a glass of milk, Ruth knew that she had better get something besides some coloring books and a box of crayons for tomorrow.

These *kinner* needed activity, and lots of it.

Drastic times called for drastic measures.

Chapter 5

Frank didn't mean to eat Daed's flannel shirt, neither. And if he did, I'm sure he's sorry.

Gregory, Age 7

In spite of his best intentions, the sun had already set when Martin returned home. The tree farm had been busy and the work had been hard. His arms were sore and his back had that old, familiar twinge in it that came from hefting trees into the trucks that arrived to take them into town to sell at the Christmas-tree lot out near Walnut Creek.

When he entered the house, everything was quiet, the complete opposite of the usual mess and state of chaos he had become used to.

A note of alarm coursed through him.

After washing his hands in the kitchen, he noticed a large plate of peanut butter cookies. Resting on the stove top was a round casserole dish covered in foil. A tray of roasted potatoes lay right next to it.

And then he heard Ruth's voice floating from the hearth room. Smooth, melodic, and full of emotion, it was lovely.

It seemed that she was reading a story. Hoping she was actually reading to his children and not to herself—he'd never actually witnessed his children sitting still for very long—he followed his ears into the coziest room in the house.

And there they all were, huddled on a pile of thick quilts and blankets covering the oak floor. A pair of logs were burning in the stone fireplace. A vanilla-scented candle was burning on the mantel.

Meg was curled next to Ruth's feet. The twins were nestled in his favorite leather chair, squished in the middle of it. Their eyes were at half-mast. Sitting in front of Ruth were his two boys and Katrina. Gregory had his arms around Frank.

The scene was as pretty as a picture. Even Frank was gazing up at Ruth with soft brown eyes.

No one was arguing. No one was destroying anything. No one was complaining, or whining.

It was amazing. Truly. Practically a Christmas miracle.

"Didn't think this was possible," he mumbled to himself, though not quietly enough.

With a start, eight sets of eyes turned to stare at him.

After that tiny pause, Ruth broke the silence, stating the obvious. "Martin, you are back."

"Ah, *jah*."

"I hope you had a *gut tawg*?"

When was the last time anyone asked him about his day? Asked him anything about himself? "*Jah*," he said awkwardly. Again. "My day, it was *gut*." His gaze skittered over to his children, each of whom was looking at him in a way that made him feel like an interloper.

And because of that, he stood awkwardly in his spot. He didn't know whether he wanted to be dismissed or invited to join them.

When it was obvious that he wasn't about to divulge anything more—after all, what more could he add? Ruth spoke. "Well, now. I am glad to hear that. Our day was good as well."

"It was?" he blurted, then carefully amended his words. "I mean, um, that is *gut* news. *Wonderful-gut*."

Katrina wrinkled her nose. "*Wonderful-gut*?"

His eldest was right. He had been a touch too enthusiastic. "I'm glad you all had a good day with Ruth."

Ruth looked amused. "Indeed. Well, I suppose since you are here I had better go." She snapped the book shut.

Thomas visibly flinched. "Hey, wait a minute!"

"What is wrong, Thomas?"

"You didn't finish the chapter!"

"You are right, but your father is here. And that means it is time for me to leave."

"But what about Scrooge? What about his ghost?"

"I guess we'll have to see if you *kinner* are interested in what happens to all of them tomorrow."

"But you don't have to leave yet, do you? I mean, you could read just a little more."

"I'm sorry, but I cannot. I need to go home. And your *daed* looks most anxious to be with you." Gazing across at him, she smiled softly, then stood and picked up her hamper. "*Gut naught, kinner.* I'll see you bright and early in the morning."

"Good-bye, Ruth," Meg said as she wrapped her arms around Ruth's knees.

After absently patting the youngest child's back, she smiled at the children and then walked to stand beside Martin.

Martin could only stare as they walked into the kitchen together. "I've never seen all six of them look so happy to be doing anything together," he said under his breath. "I've certainly never seen them all be quiet at the same time."

One eyebrow rose. "Oh?"

"They are a squirrely lot. Grace, I mean, my wife and I learned to give them a little bit of wiggle room in order for them to behave," he said.

Only after mentioning her did he realize that he'd broken his cardinal rule. He never talked about Grace. *Never.*

He braced, preparing himself to feel the usual sharp pain that came whenever he let himself think of her. Instead, all he felt was a new sense of peace.

"What did you do to them?" he asked, only half joking. And, of course, secretly wondering what she'd done to him. For the first time in months he was feeling optimistic.

"Not a thing." Looking down her nose at him— no small feat, considering she was at least six inches shorter than him. "I've only been doing what you asked me to."

"But you made supper. And cookies. And the kitchen is mopped. And they were all sitting around you on the floor. Even Frank."

"Frank goes wherever the kids go. Plus, I think we wore him out."

"You wore out the puppy?"

"*Jah.* He'll be okay, though. Don't fret. I just don't think he's used to playing tag." Ignoring his look of wonder, she continued on. "And as for the book? Well, that's no mystery. It's a good story. Everyone likes *A Christmas Carol*, I think," she said as they stopped in the mud room next to her coat. "So, would you like me to come over the same time to-morrow?"

"*Jah*. That will be just fine," he said as he watched her slip on a wool coat, red wool scarf, and mittens.

When she picked up her hamper, she gave him a little wave, then walked out the door.

"Wait! I'll go help you hitch up your buggy."

"That's not necessary."

"I'd like to help you if I could. It, ah, would be my pleasure." He had a feeling his face mirrored her confusion. Where had those words come from? He didn't usually speak like that.

Actually, he never spoke like that—not since his courting days. Maybe not even then.

When her eyes met his, they softened. Making her look even younger, and almost vulnerable. "*Danke*," she replied, just as he heard a crash from the other room.

Martin grimaced. "One second." Rushing to the door of the hearth room, he said, "What happened?"

"Daed!" Karin called out. "Gregory touched me!"

"Did not. I stepped on her, 'cause she wouldn't move. Tell her to leave me alone."

"Make me!"

Martin groaned. Turning into the hearth room again, he glared at his sweet children who were now looking—and behaving—like their usual selves. "I will talk to each of you in a moment. But for now I'm going to help—"

"It's all right, Martin," Ruth protested from behind

him. Quickly, he turned and saw that she'd already put on a black bonnet over her *kapp*. "I don't need your help."

"But, this won't take a minute."

"I've been hitching up my buggy on my own for years now. Why don't you go see to your *kinner*?"

"But—"

"I'll be just fine. I promise."

He was about to argue when he heard yet another crash, followed by a thud and a screech. "I had better go. There's a good possibility one of them might have drawn blood by now."

Ruth gazed at him, her pretty blue eyes warm. "Good night, Martin," she said softly.

Only after he closed the door did he whisper, "And good night to you, Ruth."

Thursday-night supper at the Keim house was never a quiet affair. It never had been, what with she and Aaron having six *kinner*, Lovina supposed. Back when her own children were small, she'd kept a firm hand on them. Maybe, too firm.

When Peter married Marie, they'd taken over the main house and Lovina and Aaron had moved to the *dawdi haus*. In what had felt like no time at all, Peter and Marie had had Roman and then twin girls, Elsie and Viola.

Those had been *wonderful-gut* years. She and Aaron had loved being around Peter's children, finally getting to enjoy the children without feeling the heavy responsibility of raising them to be proper and faithful adults.

But now that all three of those grandchildren were grown? Well, things had changed quite a bit. Yet again.

Marie and Peter were having a hard time getting used to having so many quiet evenings on their own, so about three months ago, Marie had started hosting Thursday-night suppers for anyone in the family who wanted to come over. She'd told everyone that she simply wanted to see them all at least once a week.

Lovina suspected that Marie had another reason, to do with Lovina's favorite granddaughter, Elsie. Elsie and Landon were newlyweds, and Landon had a very busy job refinishing floors and consequently was gone a lot. Soon after Elsie married Landon, Peter and Marie wanted to create a way to help ease Elsie's life, given that she was now almost completely blind.

Elsie was doing much better than any of them had ever imagined she would. She had a Seeing Eye dog now, a lovely, friendly, golden retriever named Betsy who was as smart as a whip.

Now, on Thursdays, at least, Elsie and her newly-wed husband wouldn't have to worry about supper.

Just as important, the rest of the family wouldn't be besieging Elsie the rest of the week, trying to monitor how she was doing.

They were all used to looking out for her. At first, Lovina had imagined that giving Elsie more space was going to be an easy thing to do.

Instead, pulling away and letting her be more independent had been more difficult than any of them had imagined. Especially for herself. She was terribly fond of her sweet, shy granddaughter. Ironically, shy Elsie was the one who was most able to stand up to her.

Which meant that Lovina, to everyone's surprise, had been the first person to back down. Of course, Lovina had learned the hard way that no good came from trying to force her wishes on another person.

Tonight Elsie and Landon were over, as was Lovina's daughter Lorene and her husband, John Miller. Roman, his wife, Amanda, and their daughter, Regina, lived with them in the main house. While they sometimes chose to go out for supper, they were around the table, too. Marie had elected to serve a pork roast and mashed potatoes. Lorene had brought over roasted carrots and squash, and Amanda had made a peanut butter pie.

As they passed plates, conversation was lively, especially since little Regina was intent on telling her grandfather every single thing she'd done with her mother that day.

Elsie was also glowing because she'd received a letter from Viola. Landon had read it aloud to her when he'd gotten home from work. Therefore, the two of them were sharing all of Viola's news, as well as the fact that Viola and her husband, Edward, would be coming home for the holidays.

"It's going to be a wonderful, busy Christmas," Lovina said with a soft smile at Marie. "We're going to have to plan accordingly."

"I agree. With Viola coming home, our *haus* is going to be full to bursting, and we can do some of our favorite projects. Maybe we can even make some homemade bird feeders to give as gifts."

Lovina privately thought that the last thing her missionary granddaughter was going to want to do was make bird feeders. She kept that to herself, however. Lovina smiled. "Of course." She'd just taken a bite of the roast—really, Marie made a good roast—when her daughter Lorene set her silverware on her plate.

After glancing at her brother Peter, Lorene said, "Goodness, all this talk about Viola coming home almost made me forget to share my news."

"And what is that?"

"Well, I just happened to be talking to some folks at the cheese shop, and learned that Ruth Stuzmann was laid off from her new job at Daybreak."

Only with effort did Lovina keep her expression neutral.

Aaron frowned. "Who's Ruth?"

"She's that dark-haired girl I told you about," Lovina muttered to her husband under her breath.

"Gosh, I haven't seen Ruth in ages," Roman said. Turning to his wife, he said, "Ruth has kind of a sad story. For whatever reason, she was raised in various relatives' homes for most of her life. Now she lives on her own in downtown Berlin."

Amanda set her napkin down. "She's not married yet?"

"No. She's kind of an awkward gal. Not in a bad way, just a little strange."

Looking concerned and a little confused, Amanda said, "Are you close to her, Lorene?"

"Not so much. The only reason I'm sharing her news is that I heard *someone* encouraged her to go help out Martin Rhodes and his brood of children."

Lovina struggled to remain impassive as Lorene glanced her way.

John visibly winced. "Heaven help her. Martin brought all six of them into the furniture store two months ago. I thought we were going to have to close the shop in order to clean it up. They are wild children."

Elsie grinned. "Rambunctious, for sure. I watched over them for an afternoon last year when Martin had to attend a meeting downtown. Somehow they managed to spill punch all over the kitchen floor and track mud through the rest of the house." She grimaced. "And all over one of the couches."

"Which was probably why they were shopping for a new one," John quipped.

Marie grimaced. "Oh, Elsie."

Elsie shrugged. "I felt bad, especially because Martin wasn't real pleased with me about the state of his house, but what could I do? After one hour I started leaning toward self-preservation."

"Now they have a dog," Lovina said, unable to help herself. "Its name is Frank."

Lorene chuckled. "Well, of course they do. It's not like a dog is going to make a difference in their home."

John smiled. "I'm still not quite sure how either the Rhodes *kinner* or Ruth's new job is our concern. But that said, I'll be sure and keep them in my prayers tonight."

"I'm sorry," Lorene said slowly, with a new, piercing look directed at Lovina. "I forgot to tell you all the rest of the story."

"Which is?"

"Folks seem pretty sure that Ruth took this job at Mamm's urging."

Elsie's brows went up. "Mamm?"

"Mine?" Marie asked.

"Not you, Marie. My *mamm*."

Lovina squirmed as everyone at the table turned to her.

Peter's eyebrows snapped together. "Why, Mamm? Why on earth would you decide that sweet Ruth Stutzman needed to spend the month of December with the Rhodes children?"

"I don't appreciate your tone, Peter."

"I'm sure you don't. But is what Lorene said true? Did you arrange this?"

"Maybe."

"Ach, Lovina," her husband murmured. "You told me that you were going to help Martin for a few days."

"I tried, but I couldn't do it."

"Mommi *was* fairly rattled when I picked her up," Roman said.

But instead of looking concerned, her husband's voice became even quieter. "Lovina, why on earth did you coerce Ruth to go over there?"

"Coerce is putting it a bit harsh."

"Cajole?" Peter asked.

"Manipulate?" Lorene murmured.

Looking amused, Elsie raised her brows. "Wheedle?"

Lovina hadn't blushed in ages but she definitely felt her cheeks heat. "Ruth is a young girl. She needed a job. Besides, her talents were wasted in that old folk's home. As are her charms. She's a pretty girl, you know. And she's got a good heart, too."

Roman reached for the plate of rolls and placed another on his plate. "Mommi, I happen to think that any children, rowdy or not, would probably be much happier with someone besides you." Before she could comment on that, he continued. "But why would the situation be right for Ruth?" He waited two beats, then whistled low. "You aren't really thinking of matchmaking, are you?"

"Roman, just because you are a preacher now, it don't mean you have all the answers."

The corners of his mouth lifted. "I know I don't. Only the Lord has all the answers. But . . . I have a feeling that I might be right about this."

"Just for the record, I might be right about this, too," Lovina said. "Martin Rhodes needs a new wife, the *kinner* need someone to keep them in line, and Ruth needs to start living." When she paused dramatically for emphasis, everyone at the table started laughing.

"What?"

Lorene shook her head. "You know what, Mamm."

"I know I'm right about this," she repeated. "Why, I bet by Christmas they'll wonder how they ever lived apart."

Lorene sighed. "I hope you're right, Mamm. Because if they don't find peace and happiness, they will probably blame every bit of their problems on you."

Lovina opened her mouth, tried to think of a quick retort. But all she could think to say was, "Pass the rolls over here, Roman. They turned out *gut* tonight."

Chapter 6

Mamm used to say we were wonderful-gut kinner. Especially when we were sleeping.

Katrina, Age 9

Feeling like she'd just had the longest, most confusing day ever, Ruth slipped her key into the door of her apartment sometime around seven o'clock, stepped inside, and grinned broadly. "I made it!" she said into the silence.

And though, of course, no one answered her, she had never been so happy to be in her little home.

"Home" was actually a one-room apartment on the outskirts of Berlin. Years ago someone had decided to convert an old bank building into three apartments. That meant half her walls were made of red brick and the ceilings were high.

When her landlord bought the building, he made

further improvements. Each unit had a pretty fireplace lined in red brick, a kitchen large enough for two people to cook side by side, and a nice, modern shower in the bathroom.

When she'd moved in, she'd painted the walls the palest shade of pink. It was so pale that most visitors didn't realize they were standing in the midst of so much pink. But at night, when there was a fire in the fireplace and a candle burning, a warm, rosy glow illuminated the room. She thought it was beautiful.

She'd continued the pink theme by sewing a daffodils quilt, with each daffodil made up of a different shade of pink, rose, or red. Her couch was white, as were her kitchen towels, shades, and the cushions on her rocker.

It was completely feminine and pretty and clean. Ruth had always secretly believed that it was a good representation of the life she'd always wanted to have.

Especially when she was a child. Years ago, when she'd been shuffled from one extended family member to the next, she'd often dreamed of being given a beautiful, clean room all for herself. That had never happened.

Sometimes she'd been given a real bed, placed in the corner of someone's room. Once she was simply given the couch. Everyone had done the best they could, but no matter where she was, she'd never forgotten that these relatives were only being charitable.

With both her parents gone and her grandparents in poor health, she'd been forced to live with distant cousins, aunts, and—for one awful year—one of her second cousins-in-law.

When she'd turned sixteen she'd gotten work as a caregiver for an elderly lady who'd grown up Mennonite. Though she was firmly living in the English world, Jean had yearned to be around someone who spoke Pennsylvania Dutch and reminded her of the way she'd grown up.

When Ruth learned that she would be getting a generous salary, plus a little apartment in the back of the house, she'd jumped at the chance.

It had been the right decision. She'd loved living with Jean and had lived with her for four years, until Jean's health became such that her daughters moved her closer to them.

Those four years had been transformative. For the first time in her life, Ruth hadn't had to move every ten or twelve months. She'd had her own space and she lived with someone who was truly happy to see her each day.

During those four years, she'd become a friend instead of a burden. A source of happiness instead of an unwanted responsibility.

She'd saved most of her pay and used it on this apartment. From the time she'd moved in, she'd felt that it was the most perfect place in the world. She could be herself here. She didn't have to worry about pleasing other people or staying out of their way.

She could relax and be happy and simply enjoy being in her own little apartment.

And she usually did.

Until tonight.

Now it simply felt lonely and too quiet.

Walking into the kitchen, she opened a can of soup and made herself a ham sandwich. And then she pulled out her newest library book and read a chapter while eating her supper.

She was reading, wishing the time would go by faster . . . until she remembered that the Rhodes *kinner* were going to be eagerly awaiting that hamper.

Suddenly, she wasn't quite so alone. She wasn't quite so lonely. She had things to do.

So as soon as she finished, she rushed to her scrap bag and got organized.

It was late. After midnight, at least.

Martin stretched his legs, shifted, and stretched again. Then at last gave up his goal of trying to get comfortable and got to his feet.

But he still was not in any hurry to walk to his bedroom at the back of the house.

When Grace had been alive, he'd procrastinated going to bed, too. But of course that had been for a very different reason. Grace had been a bed hog. He'd used to tease her, saying that no man had ever made a mattress big enough for her slim, five-foot-two-inch frame. She'd taken quite an exception to that, of course.

But she'd never denied it. Grace had never met a middle of a bed that she didn't try to claim in her sleep.

He used to brace himself whenever he got in bed to sleep beside her. She hated to scoot over and never did it willingly. He'd finally sigh and curve an arm around her and fall asleep, deciding he'd rather rest than attempt to carve out another foot of space.

Grace had laughed about that, of course. And, in some of her more joyful moments, she used to tease him that all that cuddling was why they had six children in just about as many years.

Now that she was gone, he avoided that bed because the opposite was now true. He had altogether too much space.

He also wished he could take back all the complaints he'd uttered to her. And complain, he had. Maybe it had been the stress of owning the tree farm, or the fact that for just about seven years straight he'd never had a full night's sleep. Whatever the reason, he had often been short-tempered. Sometimes overly critical.

And now he had to live with all those regrets.

"Daed?" Katrina asked as she padded down the stairs. "What are you doing up?"

His eldest daughter really was nine going on thirty. "Nothing. What are you doing up? You are supposed to be asleep."

"I know." Her eyes flickered over to him before padding into the kitchen. "I got thirsty."

"Ah." He followed her into the kitchen, leaning against the doorjamb as she got on her tiptoes, pulled a glass off the shelf, and then poured herself some water.

It was dark. Only the dim glow of the moon, the dying embers in the fireplace, and the candle he'd lit illuminated them. But in spite of that obstacle, Katrina didn't seem to be having much of a problem seeing to her needs.

Which made him think that maybe she'd done this before.

"Do you do this often? Come down to get water?"

After swallowing, she set the glass down in the middle of the stainless steel sink. Then she nodded. "Uh-huh."

"Maybe you should keep a glass of water nearby when you go to bed?"

"Maybe. But I like coming down here."

"And why is that?"

"Gives me something to do when I can't sleep."

He ached to ask her about why she couldn't sleep, but he decided to let that wait for another day.

"Can you sleep, Daddy?"

"*Nee*. Not tonight, at least." He held his breath, mentally preparing himself to hear her ask about Grace. Mentally preparing himself to speak about Grace.

"Ruth is coming tomorrow, right?"

"*Jah*," he blurted. "I mean, I think she is."

"I hope so."

"Did you like her that much?" Martin was surprised Ruth had made such an impression.

But then he realized that he'd hardly talked about anything to the *kinner* at supper. They'd eaten that taco casserole with varying degrees of bliss, and then he'd washed the dishes with Gregory, which meant that he pretty much washed the dishes all by himself.

After that, the *kinner* went upstairs to take baths and get ready for bed. He'd eaten three of Ruth's cookies before slowly making his way upstairs to help Meg and the twins.

Never once had he thought to ask the children how their day had been. Not really.

But now that he had, Katrina was giving his question some thoughtful consideration. "I liked her a whole lot better than Miss Lovina."

"I don't think you're the only one to feel that way."

"I liked Ruth's book."

"I did, too. Well, what I heard of it."

"And I liked her taco dinner. And the cookies, too."

"Both were delicious, that is true."

"And I want to know what is in her hamper."

"What's so special about that?"

"She first asked us what we wanted to do with her. When we all said we didn't want to do anything, she said that was fine. So she wasn't going to show us what she brought."

Martin chuckled. "Which, of course, made you want to see what was inside even more, I suppose?"

Looking sheepish, Katrina nodded. "I wasn't *verra* nice to her at first."

"Maybe you'll be nicer tomorrow." Reaching out, he gently set a finger under her chin and lifted her head. "Try, please. She is doing us all a favor by being here."

"I'll try," she promised around a yawn. "Daddy, we should go to sleep now."

Picking up the candle, he nodded. "Want to use this to walk upstairs?"

"*Nee*. I'll be all right. *Gut naught*, Daddy."

Leaning close, he pressed his lips to her brow. "*Gut naught* to you, too, Katrina. Sweet dreams."

She smiled at him but didn't wish him the same.

Which made him begin to realize that maybe his inability to sleep wasn't that much of a secret after all.

Chapter 7

I like pink frosting the best.

Meg, Age 4

Day 4 of Christmas Break

"You came back!" Little Meg exclaimed the moment Ruth entered the Rhodeses' kitchen.

"I did, indeed." Taking a peak over her shoulder to see if Martin was in the room, Ruth said, "You sound mighty surprised. Were you afraid I wouldn't?"

Meg bit her bottom lip. "Gregory said maybe we were too naughty for you to want to see us again."

"I don't know why he would have said such a thing. You weren't naughty at all. I liked being with you." And that was true! They were rambunctious and noisy and busy and restless. But they were also bright and rather happy *kinner.*

And since she'd spent much of the night before trying to forget just how unhappy she'd been for most of her childhood, Ruth was willing to count their happiness as a true blessing.

Brigit joined them. "You know why Gregory said what he did?"

"*Nee*, I am afraid I do not."

"It's 'cause we all said we didn't want to do anything with you."

Little Brigit, with her light brown hair in two lopsided lumps under her *kapp*, looked so earnest that Ruth almost hugged her.

As it was, it was a bit of a struggle to act and sound as disaffected as she felt she needed to be. "That you did. But I also told you that I wanted you to be honest. There's nothing wrong with being honest."

"But I wasna honest," Karin said as she ran to her side. "I lied! I do like you."

Ruth was wondering how to best smooth over the outburst when their father entered the room.

And then, just as if someone had lit a fire in the room, Ruth felt energized. Immediately, her gaze turned to Martin.

And what a sight he was, too. Thick wool pants, a white T-shirt under a blue shirt, which he'd topped with a knobby wool sweater.

He looked rugged and handsome and ready to spend another day out in the sunshine and cold. And though she knew better than to ever entertain any thoughts of him at all, Ruth kept feeling her gaze wander his way.

Luckily, she was not having the same effect on him. He looked like he was once again knee-deep in refereeing his *kinners'* squabbles.

Martin sighed. "Oh, Karin. You know better than to tell tales."

"Uh-huh. Which is why I'm being honest now. 'Cause I told you about when I was lying. Right, Ruth?"

Ruth's head was spinning; she was trying so hard to keep up. "I suppose," she answered, though actually, she wasn't exactly sure what Karin was referring to.

"Wait a minute," their father interrupted. "Why were you lying in the first place?"

"Because everyone else did."

"I wasna lying," Thomas said as he appeared from the hearth room. "I didn't want to do anything with Ruth."

"Thomas, enough of that kind of talk."

"Daed, I'm not doing anything wrong right this minute. I'm telling the truth, which keeps turning from a good to a bad thing."

"Oh, brother," Martin said.

The chuckle she heard behind her made her feel surprisingly happy. Glancing at Martin again, the man was shaking his head in mock frustration.

"Ruth, is it any wonder I'm exhausted at the end of every day?"

Before she remembered that she was there to cook and clean and get paid, Ruth met his eyes. "I'm starting to wonder how you ever manage to get out of bed in the morning!"

His green eyes warmed, too. And for a brief moment, Ruth felt a connection, the likes of which she'd never experienced before. Right that moment, it was the two of them against this rambunctious group of *kinner.*

And the idea that a strong man like him would even need her help? Well, it made her giggle. Hastily, she slapped her hand over her mouth. "I'm sorry. Well, I do believe since I did come back and you all do seem to want to do something with me . . . we should get started."

The last holdout, Katrina, appeared and maneuvered her way to the kitchen table. "Does that mean you've brought your hamper again?"

"It does, indeed." Ruth picked it up and set it on the table with a bit of a grunt. "But it's still early, and it looks to me like we need to have a hearty breakfast first." Looking at Martin, she said, "Have you eaten?"

He looked taken aback. "Me?"

His reaction made her smile. "*Jah*, Martin. You. Have you eaten?"

Looking down at his feet, he muttered, "Well, not exactly."

Katrina tilted her head. "Are you lying now, Daed?"

"Not at all. It's just that I don't have much time. . . ."

"I'm sure you have time for eggs and toast and maybe some ham?"

"I don't know if we have any ham. . . ."

"I brought my own."

"You brought your own ham?" Martin asked.

"Well, yes. You don't mind, do you?"

Staring at her like she confused him as much as the children were confusing her, Martin shook his head slowly.

"I bought the ham the other day. It was on sale, you see. But I started thinking that one ham would go to waste on a single girl like me."

"So you brought it here to us?"

"*Jah*," she said as she reached in and pulled out the smoked ham. When the *kinner* clapped, Ruth felt herself blush. "It's better to share, I think."

"It came out of the basket!" Meg cried. "It's a fancy basket!"

"It is fancy, but there's nothing too special about me bringing ham. I simply had it at home, and I didn't want it to go to waste," she explained as she bustled over to the pans, lit one of the gas burners, and started slicing the meat.

"*Kinner*, I have much planned for us today. That

means I need your help so I can make your father a good breakfast. Quick now, help me get out the eggs and milk and butter. Martin, would you like a fresh cup of coffee, too?"

"*Nee.* I mean, I already had some coffee. And there's no reason for you to—"

"Sit down, Martin," she interrupted. "But don't take a peek inside that hamper. Children, keep an eye on your father now."

Their father looked flummoxed. "I don't understand. . . ."

Playfully, she shook a finger at him. "You heard what I said. You have to be patient, just like everyone else." Her heart started beating wildly as she realized what she'd just blurted to her new employer.

But to her amazement—and the children's—he sat. Then he accepted the cup of coffee she handed him.

As the children wandered out of the kitchen, a new tension filled the air. It was compounded by the fact that Martin kept staring at her.

Staring at her in such a way that she began to wonder if maybe, just maybe, she hadn't missed out on every opportunity to claim some adventure and happiness for herself.

Maybe, just maybe, the Lord had simply been biding His time until this year.

When she returned Martin's gaze, she felt a tingle dance along her spine. It took a minute, but she recognized what that little tingle was. It was that same feeling she'd felt when Jonas Miller smiled at her.

That feeling of hope, of giddy excitement. That feeling that everything wonderful and special was within her grasp. All she had to do was reach out for it. As her mind spun, she slowly became aware that Martin was gazing at her with more than a little amusement. And more than a little bit of confusion.

"Ruth, are you all right?"

"Of course," she blurted. And she was. All she had to do was get her head wrapped around the idea that something special was happening. And that Martin was feeling it, too.

"Miss Ruth, I think your special ham is burning!" Thomas exclaimed when he came running back into the kitchen.

"What? Oh, no!" Quickly she turned and pushed the pan from the burner.

Gregory drew to a stop next to him and peered in the pan and wrinkled his nose. "Is it supposed to look like that?"

"Nope," Thomas answered.

After treating the boys to a stare, Ruth examined the ham. "It's a little crisp, but it will be all right."

As the rest of the children returned to the kitchen, Ruth cleared her throat. Turning back to their father, she added, "I think it's going to be all right, after all."

Something new flashed in Martin's eyes.

Reminding Ruth that she'd been talking about something much more than a slice of ham—and that Martin realized it as well.

He needed to get out of the kitchen, Martin realized. For some reason, he couldn't seem to keep his eyes off her, and she was aware of that.

And because she was aware of him, he'd managed to make his new babysitter uncomfortable. It was as obvious as if she'd suddenly pulled a stop sign from her basket and flashed it in front of his face.

The right thing would be to quietly excuse himself. To walk out of the kitchen and give her some space. Let the children enjoy her attentions.

But for the life of him, he couldn't do that. Not just yet. For the first time since his wife passed away, his imagination had been sparked. He wanted to know more about her. He wanted to watch her with his children, see what she did to make them so happy. Try to figure out why just watching her help his children smile made *him* so happy.

He even wanted to know what else she had in that wicker basket. And if she was going to read more of her book that afternoon.

As she continued to make his breakfast—the breakfast that he hadn't asked for and didn't really want—Martin knew he needed to do something very soon. He could already tell that his children thought he was acting strangely.

Therefore, for the good of everyone, he pushed back his chair and stood up. "You know what? I should probably—"

"I brought everything to play Christmas Bingo," she blurted as she put a plate filled with two fried eggs and a well-done slice of ham in front of him. "That's what's in my basket."

Six sets of eyes stared at her. And he? Well, he eased back in his chair and picked up a fork. "Pardon?"

She opened the hamper and pulled out seven cardboard squares. Each square already had the letters B-I-N-G-O neatly printed at the top of the card. Below the letters was a carefully drawn grid.

Each of the children picked up a card and looked at it curiously.

Then they looked at their father for answers. But he didn't have any. He was just as much at sea as they were.

"What are we supposed to do with these?" he asked after he ate a forkful of eggs.

"You need to draw pictures, of course," she explained as she dove right back into the hamper.

Once again, all of the children leaned slightly forward, watching as she pulled out a large sheet of paper with a variety of pictures drawn on them. And then she pulled out two containers of fine-tip markers.

"After we have breakfast, everyone is going to draw these pictures on their cards."

"Huh?" Gregory asked.

"You're designing your own Bingo card, silly," Ruth said, just as if it was a normal daily occurrence. Or a time-honored Amish Christmas tradition.

It wasn't, of course. As far as he knew, the Amish most definitely did not play Christmas Bingo.

"Daed?" Katrina asked. "Have you done this before?"

"Never. And what's more, I'm not sure that—"

"My friend Jean taught it to me," Ruth interrupted. "I lived with her four years and she taught me all sorts of fun games. Christmas Bingo will be fun. I promise."

"Are you sure?" Katrina asked.

"Positive," Ruth replied.

Still the *kinner* were looking at Martin, trying to figure out if they should accept her game or not.

But before he could decide one way or the other, Ruth shook her head as she picked up her hamper and set it on the floor. "You all are incorrigible. And you've seriously neglected your notion of fun."

"We . . . We've had fun before."

"That's up for debate, since you have no idea what Christmas Bingo is."

Thomas looked flummoxed. Almost speechless. This was such a rare event that Martin was tempted to write the date down.

Instead, he stood up again. He was too tempted to never go to work. He was as tempted as his children to be cast under Ruth's spell.

But he had to stay strong. "Breakfast was *gut*. *Danke*. But I need to go. Now."

Karin tugged on his shirt. "But, Daed, you were going to make a Bingo card with us."

"I wish I could, but I must go tend to the trees," he said as he crossed the kitchen and grabbed another slice of ham off the paper towels.

Ruth picked up his plate. "But what about your breakfast? You barely touched anything."

"I'll be fine. Good-bye for now."

"Good-bye for now, Martin," Ruth said.

He turned to the children, ready to give them last-minute hugs. Ready to warn, cajole, and bribe them to be good. To promise them that he would be able to take a couple of weeks off after Christmas.

But not a one of them was paying the slightest attention to him.

Instead, they were all staring at the Bingo cards and looking at Ruth like she was the most amazing thing they'd ever seen.

Only when he got to the barn did it occur to him that his children were probably right on the money.

It seemed Ruth Stutzman, all five-feet-four inches of her was a force to be reckoned with.

His family's very own miracle worker.

Chapter 8

I'm a good artist, and Karin is, too.

Brigit, Age 5

The door slammed behind Martin with a resounding *clank*, making Ruth feel as if Martin hadn't just been saying good-bye for the day, but good-bye to everything that she'd been imagining had started between them. His departure created a gap in the room, as if the central focal point had been removed.

Not that she should even care.

And in the space that remained, all that was left was the startling rush of silence.

It made Ruth shiver. Gazing at the children, she summoned a smile, even knowing while she did, that it was patently fake. "Well, now," she murmured. "I guess it's just the seven of us again. Are you ready for breakfast?"

Thomas blurted, "How come Daed left? Did that make you sad?"

"Not at all," she lied. "I was hired to take care of all of you, not keep tabs on your father."

Katrina's eyebrows snapped together. "But he didn't eat breakfast."

"He was in a hurry, that's all. I bet lots of folks are wanting to buy trees."

Staring at her father's neglected plate, Katrina shook her head. "I don't think Daed was worried about a bunch of trees."

Ruth didn't think so, either, but she sure wasn't going to start guessing why he suddenly hadn't been able to run out of the kitchen fast enough. "Don't make mountains out of molehills. Your father is fine. And you are, too."

Katrina turned to Thomas. "You know what? It's almost like he didn't want to leave today."

He scrunched his nose. "I don't know, Kat. He ran out of here pretty quick-like."

"I'm sure he simply remembered he had something important to do," Ruth said, attempting to smooth things over. "Or perhaps there is a concern at work none of you know about. That happens."

Thomas kept staring at the door. "Maybe. But I don't know."

"Daddy really likes work," Karin blurted.

"*Jah,*" Katrina replied after glancing at the door again. " 'Cause work is really important, you know."

That was a leading statement if Ruth had ever heard one. It practically was begging for her to smooth it over. Unfortunately, she was no expert when it came to the correct way to handle things of this nature. She hadn't grown up with a family, and she'd certainly never had a close relationship with a man. Well, not close enough to have the occasion to counsel him or to coax him to behave in a certain way.

Though right at that moment, she wished she had.

"Now that your *daed* left, it's time for you *kinner* to eat. Everyone sit down and I'll make you some breakfast."

Ruth hustled over to the stove and began pouring pancake batter onto the griddle and transferring slices of ham onto plates. Without being asked, the children helped. Empty Bingo cards were set aside, forks and spoons were laid out. Orange and apple juice and a pitcher of milk was pulled out of the refrigerator.

Syrup was warmed in a small pan.

Then, not twenty minutes after their father had rushed out of the kitchen like his feet were on fire, the children had their heads bowed in silent prayer.

Ruth's was, too. And though she took care to convey her thanks to the Lord for healthy food and healthy children, she also asked Him for a good dose of strength and wisdom. It was becoming a little obvious that she was out of her element with both the *kinner* and their father.

Soon, everyone dug in, the children eating the pancakes like they were something special. And little by little, the tension that had been in the room like it was a tangible thing, slowly eased. And when that happened, Ruth felt her shoulders relax. She hadn't even known they were tense.

"I like your pancakes, Ruth," Brigit said.

"I am glad."

"Me, too," Karin said.

"I'm glad about that, too. That makes me happy."

When they were almost done, Brigit spoke again. But this time it seemed like she was talking more to her siblings than to Ruth. "Maybe we did something we weren't supposed to. Maybe that's why Daddy left in such a hurry."

Karin stared at her twin. "I haven't been naughty lately. Have you?"

Brigit shook her head. "Not since I washed Frank in Daed's bathtub and then he dried off by rolling around on top of Daed's bed."

"I've been almost good," Gregory declared. "Most of the time."

Ruth looked from one to the other and tried very hard to keep her smile hidden. "It sounds like you've given your father quite a few headaches over the years. Is that the case?"

Katrina bit her lip, though the new brightness in her eyes sparkled a bit. "Maybe."

"Why is that?"

"We don't try to be bad, Ruth," Thomas replied. "It's just that sometimes we get tired of trying to be good."

Maybe Ruth was going crazy, but for some reason that made sense to her. At the moment, it kind of sounded like her life. For most of her days, she'd tried her best to be positive and make the best of things. Tried to be happy about living alone. Tried to live each day giving thanks instead of wishing for more.

No matter how difficult her days might have been, she'd gotten through them by reminding herself that they could be worse.

But now she was starting to realize that it was okay to want more. After all, the Lord started each day with a new dawn. Surely that meant He gave each of them opportunities to make each day better than the last. And maybe even to try to obtain things they wanted.

She'd always wanted to feel needed and like she belonged. These children, these rambunctious, restless, silly, imperfect *kinner* were helping her to remember that it was okay to want more.

All of that was why she looked at Thomas and started grinning. And then, well, she threw back her head and laughed.

"If it's going to be this cold, we might as well have snow," Martin's partner, Floyd Miller, commented as they pruned another group of trees and loaded the boughs into the back of a cart.

Martin, Floyd, and a couple of their part-time workers would then spend the next couple of hours fashioning the limbs into wreaths and garlands.

That was an easy job, and a warm one, too, considering Martin took care to make sure they had gas-powered heaters in the metal building.

But that seemed like a long time away, considering he and Floyd were at the top of the hill and feeling each gust of wind with every inch of their bodies.

"You have a point, but the snow would make things harder."

"If we had snow, we'd have sleds."

"And shoveling."

"Sales would be up. Snow puts people in the Christmas spirit."

Martin chuckled. "You have a point there. But the sales have stayed steady this year. We need to be happy with what we have."

As Floyd carefully trimmed another pair of

branches, then tossed them into the wagon, he eyed Martin. "What's going on with you?"

"Nothing."

"No, you're different. You're usually the one who is complaining or fretting."

"Maybe I didn't want to be that person today."

"Because?"

"Because of nothing."

"Hmm." Floyd cut another branch, inspected it, then added it to the pile. "How's your new babysitter working out?"

Against his will, Martin started. "Don't know. It's only her second day."

"But what do the *kinner* say? And don't say nothing because everyone knows that your children have something to say about most everything."

Martin weighed his response, then wondered why he even tried. "So far, they seem to like her."

"Who is it? Anyone I know?"

"It's Ruth Stutzman. Do you know her?"

Floyd's eyes widened. "You've got Ruth over there?"

"I guess you do know Ruth. So, um, what do you know about her?"

"Nothing."

"No, your reaction wasn't nothing. What do you know about her?"

"I know that she grew up outside of Charm."

"Oh. I knew that, too." He was curiously disappointed. Not that he wanted Floyd to pass on any dark secrets or anything, but he would have appreciated learning something new about her.

Floyd tossed another handful of branches into the wagon. "Almost full."

"Yep. We'll be ready to take this into the barn after we trim another five to ten trees."

"Did you know Ruth is an orphan?"

He stilled. "Not at all. Did she live in an orphanage or something?" Actually, he wasn't even sure if he'd ever heard of an Amish orphanage.

"She was passed from relative to relative. She usually stayed for no more than a year at a time."

"How do you know about this?"

"I'm courting Kristy who is *gut* friends with Ruth. Strange, though. I could have sworn Kristy said that Ruth had taken a job over at Daybreak with her."

"She had."

"So why is she watching your *kinner* now?"

"From what I understand, Daybreak had to lay a couple of people off. Since she was the last hired, she was the first to go."

"Tough."

"Uh-huh. Plus, after Lovina didn't exactly work out, I think she felt like she needed to find me someone. So I think she convinced Ruth to take the job."

Floyd backed up a step and pretended to shiver.

"Say no more. I've lived my life hoping Lovina won't ever know who I am."

"She's not that bad."

"Yes, she is." He grinned. "Even Roman says so."

"Really? Roman is her grandson."

"He would know." Floyd walked to the next tree, eyed it carefully, then set to pruning. "Is Ruth planning to watch your *kinner* for a while?"

"Just until New Year's Day. Then the *kinner* will go back to school and maybe by then Daybreak'll be hiring again, and they can take her back." But even as he said that, he felt a bit sad about it. Ruth was a chatty girl. Full of energy. From his kids' response that morning, he knew she was doing a great job with them She'd won them over in just one day, which was quite a feat.

It seemed a waste for her to go back to the retirement home. A girl like her, so vibrant and full of life, should be surrounded by a doting husband and a bunch of children of her own.

"What do you think about that?"

He shrugged. "There's nothing to think about. It is what it is. For right now, I've been blessed with help."

"If she came back for a second day, it means your children haven't run her off yet."

"There is that." Martin grinned. "It sure is a shame that Kristy wasn't available to help me out."

"Kristy is a delicate soul. She's adorable and loving."

Martin knew what was coming. "And?"

"And the thought of just looking out for your Katrina alone intimidates her. There's no way she'd want to tackle six of them."

"Floyd, you know my children."

"I do know them."

"And I am grateful for my many blessings. I love them. Very much."

"I know that, too."

"That said, I don't blame Kristy one bit."

Floyd grinned as he tossed two more branches into the wagon. "It takes a strong man to be honest about his children, Martin."

"Then I must be the strongest man in town," he replied dryly.

Sobering, Floyd reached out and slapped Martin lightly on the back. "Grace died too young."

"That she did. She died too young," he repeated as they set their tools in the wagon, then helped guide the horse down the hill. She died too young and took his heart with her.

He'd always been sure of it.

Which was why he couldn't understand why he kept thinking about Ruth's smile. Or her blue eyes.

Or the way he'd been as happy as his children to see her.

Chapter 9

I think I've grown a whole inch this month.
Maybe two. I'm almost sure of it.

Thomas, Age 8

It was early in the morning. So early that Elsie's husband, Landon, hadn't even had his second cup of coffee yet. Therefore, Elsie knew it was the perfect time to talk to him about something she'd been considering for a couple of weeks.

Now, if she could only get up the nerve. Feeling nervous and more than a little bit awkward, she reached down and gave Betsy a pet. Betsy raised her head. When she realized that Elsie wasn't about to give her a command, but was simply giving her some attention, she put her head back down on her paws.

Elsie leaned back in her chair and sighed.

"Elsie, what's going on?"

"Is it that obvious?"

"It is." Pushing his coffee cup to one side, he leaned toward her. "Is something wrong?"

"No. I just wanted to talk to you about something."

"Well, then . . ." He reached for her hand and gave it a squeeze.

And that made Elsie reflect again about just how blessed she was to have a husband like him. Now that she could hardly see at all, he often squeezed her hand or patted her shoulder, touching her in a hundred ways to show his support.

"Landon, I've been thinking about my mother's Thursday suppers."

"And . . ."

"And, while I appreciate everything she's doing, I'm a little frustrated with them." She hated to sound so ungrateful, but she knew if she held her tongue, things would only get worse. "I'm getting the feeling my mom would serve me every meal if she could."

After a pause, he chuckled. "I fear you are right about that."

"You understand?"

"Of course I do. Your family has always wanted to take care of you. Sometimes I fear that they are having a harder time adjusting to your blindness than you are."

His words were so perfect, exactly everything that she'd been thinking. She felt like raising her hand in jubilation. "That is why I wanted to do something this Christmas—if you are okay with it."

"What do you want to do?"

"I want to have Viola and Edward stay with us when they come into town."

"Sure, honey. That's no problem."

"There's more. I want Viola and me to host Christmas dinner, too."

"Here?"

She nodded. "It's time, don't you think? We're married now, and Viola and Edward are, too."

"But it's a lot of responsibility. And Elsie, I don't want to hurt your feelings, but it isn't like you can do a lot of the cooking."

"I can operate a stove and plan a menu," she replied, realizing as she did that her feelings, actually, weren't hurt. She'd come to terms with her blindness, and because of that, she didn't spend her time mourning what she couldn't do. Instead, she chose to spend her time focusing on what she still could. "I can still set a table and ask everyone to bring a dish."

She felt his warm approval float over her. And that warmth meant as much to her as a tender smile would have meant a couple of years ago.

Then he pressed his hand to the back of her neck. "Your mother isn't going to like this," he warned.

"I know."

"And your grandmother? She's going to have something to say about this, too."

"I know. But I want to at least try. Do you mind terribly?" she asked. "If you really don't want everyone to come over here, we don't have to do it."

"Actually, I think it's a great idea, Elsie," he said as he stood up. "I think you should call Amanda and get her and Roman on your side. Then, when Viola arrives tomorrow, we can break it to them that we'd like them to stay here with us."

"I hope they'll say yes."

Chuckling, he pressed his lips to her brow before he stepped toward the door, obviously ready to get to work. "I'll talk to my brother at work. You give Edith a call, too."

"Okay." She nodded, already making a mental note to ask her sister-in-law to be in charge of the turkey and stuffing.

"I'll call you in a few hours, Elsie," he said as he opened the door.

"*Danke*, Landon."

"Anytime. Anytime at all."

Once the kitchen door shut, she sat back in her favorite kitchen chair, reached down, and gave her Seeing Eye dog another gentle pat. "Today is a *wonderful-gut* day, Betsy," she murmured. When Betsy replied by thumping her tail against the hardwood floor, Elsie knew her dog couldn't agree more.

The knock at their door at two in the afternoon came as a bit of a surprise. Lovina looked at Aaron, who, until just a second before, had been staring into his coffee cup.

"I wonder who that could be?" she asked. "No one in the family knocks before coming on in."

"Maybe they've finally learned some manners," he grumbled.

She got to her feet and walked across their narrow kitchen. "Hush, now," she said before she opened the door.

And then stood staring at their beautiful grand-daughter Viola. And the teenager who was holding her hand. The girl had dark brown hair, matching eyes, and was very slender.

"Hi, Mommi!" Viola said as she practically bounded into the house. "Hi, Dawdi!"

Aaron got up from his chair and enfolded Viola in a warm hug as Lovina stood there dumbfounded. "Vi, we didn't think you were coming home until tomorrow."

"We got an earlier flight." She grinned. "Edward said we're probably the first people ever to experience better-than-expected plane flights," she said as she reached over and hugged Lovina, too.

Lovina chuckled. "Maybe so." After shuttling Viola and the girl inside, she closed the door. "Now, who do you have here?"

"I'm sorry. This is Annie."

"Hello, Annie," Lovina said politely.

Annie didn't say a word. She only stared at Lovina for a long moment before shifting her gaze to Aaron.

As the silence lengthened, Lovina raised her eyebrows at her granddaughter. This girl was frightened, Lovina realized.

"She's a little shy," Viola explained as she rested her hand on Annie's arm.

There is a story here, Lovina realized, with a bit of trepidation settling in her stomach. Knowing everything would be explained in time, she pointed to the kettle on the stove. "Dawdi and I were just having some *kaffi*. Would you like some? Or perhaps some hot chocolate?"

"That sounds great, doesn't it, Annie? We'll have some hot chocolate." Softening her voice, Viola said, "Dear, why don't you sit down, and I'll help my grandmother."

To Lovina's consternation, Annie hesitantly pulled out a chair and sat on the edge of it, almost as if she feared the wooden seat was going to take a bite out of her backside.

More confused than ever, Lovina shared a look with Aaron before shooing Viola to the table. "I don't need any help. You sit with Dawdi and your, ah, guest."

Viola sat. As Lovina started heating water and getting out her special hot-chocolate mix, Viola finally started explaining herself. "Annie is the daughter of one of the other missionaries in Belize."

"It must be so exciting to live in Belize," Lovina said.

When Annie didn't respond, Viola said, "I think it's had its times of highs and lows."

Lovina thought that sounded cryptic. "Well, I'm sure you and your parents will find an Ohio Christmas far different from the ones in Belize."

While Annie's cheeks heated, Viola rushed to explain. "Actually, Annie didn't come here with her parents. Just me and Edward."

"Oh?"

"*Jah.* Her father elected to stay in Belize for Christmas," Viola said lightly. "And Annie hasn't had a mother for a long time."

"I see." After glancing at Annie again, Lovina poured hot water into the prepared mugs. After stirring both, she placed two of her famous homemade marshmallows on top of each and set them in front of the girls. "Well, I am certainly sorry to hear that you will be away from your father at Christmas, but I am mighty glad you have joined us."

"Me, too," Viola said.

After placing a plate of homemade Christmas cookies on the table, Lovina joined them. "Annie, I hope you like noisy families, because things have been especially noisy around here lately, what with Christmas just around the corner."

A new shadow entered Viola's eyes. "Actually, Mommi, that's why we are here."

"And why is that?"

"Well, Edward and I stopped by to see Elsie before we got here. I couldn't wait to see my twin, you know."

Lovina was surprised that Viola had paid Elsie a quick visit, but she supposed she shouldn't have been. The twins had always had a special bond. "Yes?"

"Elsie asked if Edward and I would stay with them." Eyes lighting up, she added, "Elsie wants to host Christmas dinner."

"That's impossible."

Viola shook her head. "I don't think so. Amanda and I are going to help her. The three of us are going to host the supper at Elsie's *haus*."

"Does Marie know about this?"

"I don't know. Elsie was going to call Mamm, and Roman and Amanda were going to go over and talk to her, too."

Lovina's head was spinning. "This makes no sense," she blustered. "Elsie's home is mighty small. And . . . And she's blind, Viola."

After a careful glance Annie's way, Viola said, "She knows she's blind, Mommi. But see, I think that's why we need to all offer to help her instead of pushing aside her wishes."

Lovina glanced over her shoulder at Aaron, who was sitting in his chair and pretending to read the newspaper but was really listening to every word. When he raised his chin and his brows, she realized that he agreed with Viola.

"All right then," she said weakly. "What do you think I should do?"

"I'm hoping you can do a couple of things."

"I can roast the turkey, I suppose, but it's going to be quite a chore bringing a hot turkey over to Elsie's."

"Edward and I were hoping you and Dawdi could let Annie stay here with you."

"But she is your guest."

"*Jah*. But Elsie's *haus* isn't all that big."

Aaron, who had been sitting quietly this whole time, glanced Annie's way. "Viola, perhaps you could speak to us privately for a moment. If you don't mind."

Viola's expression fell. "Oh. Of course."

Lovina stood up. "Why don't we go into my sewing room," she suggested gently, not wanting their "guest" to feel any more uncomfortable than she already did.

When the three of them were in the privacy of her sewing room, Lovina and Aaron faced their grand-daughter. "Viola, it is wrong of you to simply bring a girl over here and announce that she'll be staying with us," Aaron said.

Lovina nodded. "You should have asked us first," she whispered. "Once more, you know that, too, dear granddaughter."

Viola hung her head. "I know."

"Then you must know that we are not happy with your actions," Lovina added.

"Mommi, I didn't have any choice."

"Of course you did," Aaron retorted. "Now you aren't giving us any choice."

Viola folded her arms over her chest. "So you want to say no?"

Yes, Lovina did. But how could she say that? "I didn't say that."

"You don't need to, it's written all over your faces," Voila said. "And I must say, I'm pretty disappointed in you. It's Christmas; you're supposed to open your house to family and friends."

"She is neither. She is a stranger."

"She is in need of some kindness and a Christmas to remember," Viola retorted in a hushed voice filled with purpose. "You don't know what her life is like. Her father puts everyone and everything before her. Always. The moment he heard that a family had lost their baby and two other children were sick, he volunteered to stay with them, help dig their new well, and help take care of the children, too. He was going to make Annie do that as well."

Reaching out, she grasped Aaron's arm. "Please say you'll look after Annie and let her stay with you. I'll be with her during the day, but with Amanda and Roman living in the main house, and Regina, too, it can get a little overwhelming. Especially for someone who is used to living alone with a very quiet father. I'm worried it might be too much for her."

"But—"

"Dawdi, please say yes. Annie needs you and Mommi."

Lovina felt all the words freeze in her mouth. "Say again?"

"Mommi, she needs hugs and kindness. She needs someone to look out for her, to give her a little bit of compassion."

"And you think that is what we can give her?"

"I know it. Dawdi, you know how much I've missed you. I've missed the way you can sit with me quietly. I've missed how neither of you pretend to be anything but who you are. And because of that, you're safe. Annie won't have to walk on eggshells around you both."

Aaron ran a hand over his beard. "Don't know if you've given us a compliment or not, Viola."

Viola's cheeks bloomed. "I really want to spend some time with Elsie and help her make Christmas dinner. But I also want to take care of Annie. That's why I'm asking you both for help. Please say you'll make this a Christmas for her to remember. Please."

Lovina knew before Aaron looked her way what she was going to say. All her life, she'd been a lot of things. She'd been garrulous. She'd been in other people's business. She'd even been too cold and distant with her six children.

She'd never been praised for those things.

"You brought her here to us on purpose, didn't you?"

Viola nodded. "Annie needs my family. She needs you both more than me. Please say that is okay."

"It's more than okay," Aaron said gruffly. "Now, we should probably go back into the kitchen before she thinks we've run off."

After two quick hugs, Viola darted back to the kitchen. Then drew to an abrupt halt. "She's not here. Mommi, I think I did run her off!"

"Don't worry," Lovina replied, feeling once again like she had things in hand. "Maybe she went back to the house."

"Or maybe she's sitting on the front steps in the cold," Aaron murmured from his position at the window, nodding in that direction.

Viola reached for the handle. "I'll go—"

Feeling as if the Lord was guiding her, Lovina shook her head. "Viola, you said you had faith in us.

Maybe it's time I tried to earn that faith, *jah*?" Spying Annie's full mug of hot chocolate, she grasped that and her own mug of coffee. "Get the door for me, child. I'm going out."

"*Danke*, Mommi," Viola whispered as Lovina took a deep breath and stepped out into the cold.

Lord, please give me the right words, she silently prayed. *And, if you don't mind, maybe you could keep that up for a while, too.*

Feeling better now that she knew the Lord was fully aware of what she was going through, Lovina smiled when Annie turned to look up her way from their front steps. "I'll have you know that you gave me a start when we came back to the kitchen and we couldn't find ya."

Annie's eyes widened before she carefully concealed her feelings again. "I thought you'd be happy I was gone."

Lovina joined her on the steps, thinking as she bent down that her knees sure didn't work the way they used to.

"I'm glad you decided to talk to me. I feared the cat got your tongue."

"It wasn't that."

"I figured as much," she said lightly. "You know, I imagine you're feeling a mite awkward, being here in Ohio when you were used to being in Belize and all, but I hope you know that you're a welcome addition."

"You don't have to say that. I know you don't want company."

"I don't like my granddaughter surprising us like she did," Lovina corrected. "You may not know this about Viola, but she's an impatient person. She always has been. Actually, our Viola has a bad habit of doing things without considering the consequences. Personally, I think it's something she should work on."

Annie darted a look at her, obviously realizing that Lovina wasn't joking, and smiled softly. And just like that, her dark brown eyes lit with warmth and good humor.

Feeling like they'd come to an agreement of sorts, Lovina lifted the mug of hot chocolate she'd set on the porch. "Do you like hot chocolate?"

"I do."

"*Gut*. Then drink some."

Obediently, Annie sipped. "It's *gut*."

"It is," Lovina replied, because that was the truth. As she settled on the step, wishing she'd put on a cloak before coming outside, Lovina enjoyed the moment of silence. It looked like Annie there had the right idea. Sometimes words were not needed.

They really weren't needed at all.

Chapter 10

My teacher said I should have a pretty gut
Christmas, because I only got in trouble fifteen
times during the whole month of November.

Thomas, Age 8

For most of Ruth's life, December had been the
longest month of the year. Whatever relatives she'd
been living with had been occupied with lots of
family gatherings and all kinds of preparations. Ruth
had baked cookies and cakes right beside them.

Sometimes, she'd even gotten swept up into the
joy of the season, enjoying the decorated storefronts,
the lights on the Englischers' houses, the excited
chatter of children.

But coinciding with all the festivities was the
knowledge that Christmas Day would probably not
be a joyous one for her. Her parents weren't there to

give her hugs, she didn't have traditions to grasp hold of and to excitedly re-create year after year.

So she would exist on the outskirts of the joy. Being a part of things but not really a participant in them. And when Christmas Day did come, she would feel even more alone and disenchanted, because no matter what group of relatives she was with, she always felt like a burden.

But this year, December was passing by in a flash.

That morning when she woke up she'd realized that she'd already been going to the Rhodeses' house for a whole week. And though she was still spending time with a family not her own, with a family that would never be her own, the children didn't make her feel like that at all.

Actually, usually one or more of them would be peering out the dining room window when she arrived. They'd wave at her with bright smiles when she'd look their way.

She was greeted with hugs and chatter and, well, happiness. And, because there was no one to see, she ate up their enthusiasm like she was starved for it. Maybe she was.

They'd decorated cards and spent one whole afternoon playing Christmas Bingo for pieces of candy. Another afternoon, they'd played Candy Land.

She'd baked cookies with them and read *A Christmas Carol* and then all kinds of silly Christmas picture books she'd found at the library.

She and Martin started talking a bit more, too. Oh, they didn't talk about anything of substance, of course. But their conversations were friendly and easy. Little by little, they began to joke and tease. Finding lots of humor in the antics of his busy, sometimes rambunctious children.

And, though he probably didn't realize it, each day they talked a little bit longer. It was nice. Really nice.

Overcome by the Christmas spirit, she'd decided to celebrate by helping the *kinner* send out Christmas cards. The project would keep them all occupied for a few hours and serve another purpose, too. It would remind her that the season was what she made of it. She could either dwell on unhappy memories or remind herself that she had much to be grateful for.

Even if it was only helping six children remember that they were a family although their mother was in heaven and their father worked all the time. They were a family no matter what.

And that was something Ruth knew they would one day be grateful for.

"Do you think Daed is gonna be upset when he

sees what we're doing, Ruth?" Katrina asked when she was switching out her red marker for a blue one.

"All we're doing is making Christmas cards. There is nothing wrong with that. Nearly everyone I know sends out cards."

Katrina still looked doubtful. "But you've got out my *mamm*'s old list. My *daed* doesn't like us disturbing her things."

"I didn't go through her things, I simply happened to see it when I was flipping through her book of Christmas recipes."

"But we're not supposed to touch those, either."

The children looked so concerned, Ruth stood up. "How about this? As soon as your father gets back I'll talk to him."

"Promise?"

"I promise." She was just about to start on supper when she happened to glance Gregory's way. And noticed that his cheeks were flushed.

"Gregory?" she murmured as she reached his side. "Are you all right?"

Glassy-looking eyes rose to meet hers. "I feel like I'm getting sick."

"Uh-oh. Come into the kitchen and we'll take your temperature."

Five minutes later, the worries about disturbing Grace Rhodes's Christmas list was the least of her troubles. Not only did Gregory have a low fever and a stuffy nose and watery eyes, he also had a blister near his collar bone. And another on his back.

Struggling to keep her voice calm, Ruth said, "When did you get these spots?"

He shrugged. "I found 'em this morning."

"Ah. Do they itch or hurt?"

"Itch. Why?"

"I'm afraid you might have the chicken pox," she whispered.

"Chicken pox!" he yelled.

Which, of course, set all the children to come running. In a flash, they had surrounded Gregory and were by turns inspecting his two spots, spouting advice, and—in Thomas's case—looking a tad bit jealous.

She'd just clapped her hands to try to restore order when Martin opened the back door.

"What's going on?" he asked as he took in the chaos.

"Gregory has chicken pox," Brigit said importantly.

"Surely not."

"It's not my fault!" Gregory whined. "It just happened."

"Now, now," Ruth said, curving a hand around Gregory's shoulders. "No need to get upset. But I do think, perhaps, you should go put on your pajamas. I'll bring you some juice in a minute."

"But what about my Christmas cards?"

Martin stilled. "What Christmas cards?"

"Ruth found Mamm's old list and she is going to send everyone a card," Katrina said importantly.

"Definitely not."

Katrina's eyes turned wide. "But we've already made lots of them."

"That doesn't matter."

"But it does!" Katrina retorted. "Ruth said people are wondering what has happened to us."

Martin turned to Ruth, his eyes serious.

"We need to talk. Now."

"Yes. I think that is a very good idea." Turning to the five remaining children, she smiled softly. "How about you all clean up for me and then go sit with Gregory so he doesn't feel lonely?"

"But what about—" Thomas sputtered.

She cut him off. "Go on up, Thomas. All of you."

When the children were out of the room, Martin sank to one of the kitchen chairs and leaned his head back. "How certain are you that Gregory has the chicken pox?"

Ruth settled down in the chair across from him.

"Not a hundred percent sure, but I can't imagine what else he could have. He has two blisters and a low-grade fever."

Martin sighed and ran a hand over his head. "Every time I think I've got a handle on things, the Lord sees fit to prove me wrong."

"I don't know if it's the Lord's doing," she said gently. "I think it's just Gregory's time to get chicken pox."

"Ruth, if Gregory gets sick, they all will." His voice thickened with despair. "They're all going to be sick at Christmas and I won't be able to do a thing to help them because I've got to keep the business going."

"It will be all right."

He shook his head. "I know you mean well, but you can't possibly know what's coming. The kids told me how you grew up as an only child. I doubt you have any concept about what it means to be surrounded by so many kids, all needing one thing or another."

"You're right. I've never felt helpless and like there wasn't a single thing I could do to change things," she bit out, every word laced with pain.

He jerked his head and stared at her. Then, as it was altogether obvious that he'd caught the tinge of pain in her voice, he looked away. "Sorry. I know you've probably experienced some difficult days, but I'm feeling more than a little frustrated right now."

She shouldn't have expected him to understand what her life had been like. But though she'd surely never experienced the death of a spouse—she couldn't even begin to imagine what that had been like for him—she did, in fact, understand what it felt like to be overwhelmed by life. She'd also experienced the feeling of being weighed down and having no choice but to continue on.

She chose her words with care, staring at her hands folded in front of her. "Perhaps instead of thinking of everything that is hard, we could think of blessings."

He stilled. "Blessings?"

"*Jah*." With a small smile she said, "Though your *kinner* might soon be covered in chicken pox, you do have six of them. That is a blessing. Ain't so?"

He stiffened, then, to her relief, the corners of his lips tipped up. "That is true."

"They are *gut kinner. Wonderful-gut kinner*, Martin. And they'll get through these Christmas chicken pox." Thinking about what might be in store for them, she teased, "It might not be easy but we'll get through it together."

He looked at her, blinked.

And then, to her shock, he murmured the most incredible thing in the world. "Maybe you are more than I realized, Ruth. Maybe you are far more than either of us has ever imagined."

Though she didn't know exactly what he meant, the words were so beautiful, so loving and kind, so much everything she'd always hoped she'd one day hear but never expected to, it rendered her speechless.

At the moment, she was beyond doing anything but savoring the moment. Just for a little while.

What had he been thinking?

Staring into Ruth's blue eyes, Martin couldn't believe he'd just said something so personal. He thought he would have been smarter than that.

Feeling his cheeks heat, he inhaled. "I am sorry, Ruth. I don't know why I said such a thing. I didn't mean any disrespect."

"I didn't take offense," she said quickly.

He met her eyes again. No, she didn't look offended. Instead, she looked confused. Maybe a little flustered.

Actually, she looked a bit stunned.

And why shouldn't she? Here she'd been trying to help him, and right in the middle of their discussion, he'd let loose a fireball like that. It had been inappropriate.

Had he been so focused on his children and their needs and his troubles that he'd completely forgotten what it was like to be thoughtful of others?

His mouth went dry as he stared at her longer. It was obvious that she was aware of his scrutiny, but she didn't shy away. No, she had more of a backbone than he'd originally thought.

It ignited the tension between them. Illuminated the fact that she was prettier than he'd first realized. Her blue eyes were bluer, her curly dark hair shinier. Her cheekbones were more pronounced, her bearing softer and more feminine than he'd first imagined.

He was also realizing that she was easier to be around than he had anticipated. Almost *too* easy to be around.

The direction of his thoughts caught him off guard. Being aware of her as a woman was the very last thing on earth he needed. It wasn't right. It wasn't right to her, him, Grace's memory, or even the kids.

He needed to nip those feelings in the bud. No good would ever come out of his thinking about her as a woman.

"Um, what I meant was that I value your service."

She tucked her chin. "Yes. Yes, of course."

He felt so awkward. So foolish. "What I am trying to say is that for someone who claimed she didn't have any experience working with children, you've done a *gut* job."

"*Danke.*"

"Why, you've practically worked wonders in this house! They really like being with you. Very much so." Thinking about all the conversations that started with "Ruth said this" and "Ruth thinks that," Martin knew saying his children were going to miss her was something of an understatement.

"What would you like to do about Gregory? I fear he's going to feel worse before he gets better."

Martin figured Ruth had a point. He also had a sneaking suspicion that at least one more of the children was going to come down with the chicken pox, too. "What would you think about staying with us?" he blurted. "Until things get better?"

"You mean . . . . You mean, with all of you overnight?"

Thinking quickly, he nodded. "We already have an extra room. You can have it." Pretending he felt more excitement for the idea than he actually did, he attempted to smile.

A look of dismay passed through her eyes, though she hid it quickly. "I don't know."

"I'd pay you for your time, of course." He didn't know how, but he'd figure out some way.

"Believe it or not, it's not the money."

"What then?" He supposed she might have many reservations about staying at his house. And maybe even justifiably so. But just as important, he had a feeling that he needed to pin her down right away. Otherwise there was a very good possibility that he was going to lose her.

"I don't think it would be proper."

"How so?"

When she blushed, the reasons hit him square on the nose. "Ruth, you aren't worried that I would behave improperly, are you?"

"No, not exactly. It's just that we are both unmarried."

"Technically, that is true. But we would have half a dozen children acting as chaperones."

"That is true."

"And don't worry. I haven't the slightest wish to compromise you," he said in a rush as a smile played on his lips. "Actually, I hadn't even thought about you in such a way. Ever."

She inhaled sharply. "Of course not."

Taking another look at her, his smile faded as he saw that his honesty, delivered without the slightest hint of finesse, had been a little too blunt. Perhaps even rude.

But how did one repair that?

"Listen, I'm going to go," she said in a rush. "I'll think about your offer tonight and give you my answer in the morning."

And that was the best he could hope for, he realized. "What should I do about Gregory?"

"Cool baths, mix up some baking soda and water and make a paste to put on his blisters. Give him some children's Tylenol if his fever gets worse."

"You sound so sure."

"I've been around chicken pox a time or two. You might buy some Calamine lotion at the pharmacy. That'll help with the itching." After sliding her arms into her coat, she slipped her black bonnet on over her *kapp*. Finally, she pulled out two royal-blue mittens. "I better go now. I have plans for this evening."

"Oh. Of course. Sorry. I forget the rest of the world has a life."

"You have a life, Martin Rhodes. You have a mighty nice one," she said softly. "I'll see you tomorrow."

"I'll help you with your horse."

"Not tonight. I mean, I don't mind the chore, and you need to see to the *kinner. Gut naught*, Martin."

"Good night, Ruth," he said quietly as he watched her close the door behind her.

Alone in the kitchen, he turned to the window and watched her walk sedately toward the barn. Her chin was tucked into her chest, though whether it was to shield her face from the winter weather or because she was deep in thought, he didn't know.

When she entered the barn, he was left to simply stare at the gray skies and brown land. Land that looked as desolate as he felt inside, he realized some-what fancifully.

What am I doing, Lord? he asked silently. *What do You want me to do? I want to do Your will, but it would be kind of nice if You every now and again gave me the benefit of the doubt and You didn't try to cut me off at my knees.*

"What do you think she's gonna do?" Katrina asked from the hallway.

"Were you eavesdropping?"

"Nee."

"Sure about that?"

"I wasn't. I mean, I didn't mean to." Still stand-ing in the doorway, she said, "I was coming in to get Gregory some water and I heard you and Ruth talking."

"You should have made yourself known."

"I would've, except you sounded so serious." A line formed between her brows. "Do you think she'll come back tomorrow?"

"*Jah.*" Of that, he had no doubt.

"Do you think she'll stay here with us?"

"I don't know that answer."

"But we need her."

"I know," he said softly. "But we can't always put our needs in front of others'. Her feelings matter, too."

"But what else could be important to her?"

"That's probably the problem, don't you think? Until this very moment, I've been so focused on my selfish wants and needs I've forgotten that she has her own wants and needs, too."

Walking to his side, Katrina unconsciously mimicked his position, standing in front of the window and looking just as forlornly outside.

"I still miss Mamm."

"I know. I still miss her, too."

"I don't think the twins remember her anymore."

"It's been two years. They weren't even four when she died. You were seven. That's a big difference."

"Are you mad that they don't remember?"

"Not at all."

"But—"

"Life goes on. Go get Gregory's water. I'll be up to check on him in a minute."

For once, she followed directions without an argument. When she was out of sight, Martin stared at the empty scenery outside again and realized that it was time for him to stop.

He needed to stop wishing for snow. Stop wishing for customers. Stop wishing for time.

God was already giving him a new day each morning. To continually ask for more?

It was a selfish thing to do. He should feel ashamed.

Chapter 11

Frank only throws up when he eats too many cookies.

Gregory, Age 7

It wasn't exactly easy having a shy houseguest. But that said, Lovina was enjoying having Annie in her home more than she ever thought she would. Maybe that was because Annie was every hostess's dream— quiet and polite. Neat and respectful. Privately, Lovina thought that this girl could give lessons to most folks about the importance of good manners. Especially some of her grandchildren.

But all that aside, what really drew Lovina to their slim, timid houseguest was the fact that Annie seemed to prefer being around her and Aaron.

She and Aaron had noticed it the first time the three of them had entered the main house and joined everyone for supper. Annie had smiled shyly and spoken when she had no choice, and almost looked comfortable around Viola and Edward.

But she completely relaxed when she was near Lovina and Aaron. She chatted more, smiled more. And seemed to appreciate doing the simplest things with them, such as folding towels or sweeping the wooden floor.

She also enjoyed working on a thousand-piece puzzle with Aaron. She'd sip tea and concentrate on putting the pieces together with a focus that would have been slightly alarming if she didn't look so happy about doing it.

They had just returned from another long meal at the main house, one that involved Edward, Roman, and Landon chatting with Peter about their jobs and joking about basketball games, and the women making plans for Christmas dinner at Elsie's *haus*. Annie was seated at the kitchen table and working on the puzzle again.

When Aaron went to see if he could help with the animals in the barn, Lovina heated up some apple cider and settled across from the girl.

"You seem to like puzzles a lot," she said. "Do you do them in Belize?"

Annie popped her head up and for a moment stared at Lovina as if she'd made a joke. *"Nee."*

"Is it because no one has any? If that's the case, we

can send you back with a good supply. Or we can mail them to you, if you'd rather."

"That's mighty kind of you."

"It's nothing. Just puzzles."

Annie bit her lip. So much so, that it was obvious that she was contemplating how much to share with Lovina.

"I do enjoy puzzles, but you shouldn't mail me any. I wouldn't be able to use them."

"Oh? Why not?"

"My father, uh, he wouldn't be pleased with me wasting time like this," she finally said, brushing a tendril of dark brown hair that had gotten loose of its pins off the back of her neck.

Annie's comment had warning signs all over it. The only problem was that for the life of her, Lovina couldn't figure out what was so wrong about doing a puzzle.

With this in mind, she navigated her way carefully. "We all need to keep busy, of course. And, to be sure, being a missionary and serving God's children is a blessing. But everyone could use something fun to do, I think." Remembering how Viola said that Annie's father seemed to put the people he was serving ahead of his family, Lovina asked, "What do you usually do when you have spare time?"

Annie shrugged. "Sleep. Clean."

"*Nee.* I meant when you are simply relaxing. Enjoying the day."

"My *daed* doesn't believe in that."

He didn't believe in relaxing? "Do you have siblings?" she asked slowly. Surely there was some joy in the girl's life.

"I do. An older brother and sister."

"Are they in Belize with you?"

"*Nee*, they are back in the States, but we don't talk much. They're much older and had a falling-out with our father. Daed doesn't permit me to write to them."

Lovina ached to pry, to ask why Annie wasn't moving heaven and earth to spend time with them, but she feared she might be pushing too much if she did so. Therefore, she simply nodded in a concerned way. "Ah."

For the first time in their acquaintance, Annie's eyes brightened. "*Jah.* That just about sums it up, I think. When it comes to my family, there isn't much to say, I'm afraid."

"I am sorry for that."

"Me, too." She shrugged. "That was why when Viola asked if I'd like to come here to Ohio with her and Edward, I jumped at the chance. I may never get another opportunity to have a Christmas like this."

The girl's words humbled her, and Lovina had long since reached the age when she was sure she couldn't be humbled by much. This girl's wants were so simple, her life so empty of joy, that Lovina ached to change things.

"Is there anything I can do?"

"Pardon?"

"You might not know this, but I have something of a reputation for getting things done. And, uh, for helping others." Guiltily, she thought about Ruth and the way she'd manipulated her to help the Rhodes family. Yes, she got things done and was reasonably good at getting folks to bend to her will.

"How old are you, child?"

"Nineteen."

"How long have you been in missionary work?"

"All my life."

"It isn't my place to say this, but I'm wondering if the Lord would understand if you wanted to do something for yourself now. If your heart is in Belize and your good works there, that would be one thing. But if, perhaps, you have maybe thought about doing something else, I would encourage you to do that and talk to your father about your wishes."

Twin splotches of red bloomed in her cheeks. "I don't know what to say."

"There's nothing you need to say. Just think about it."

Annie tucked her chin in to her chest. "Lovina, my problem isn't that I want a change. My problem, I fear, is that I don't even know what to wish for."

Lovina was thinking of her own past, of how she'd made a series of bad decisions when she was a teenager and then kept her past a secret for almost forty years. Of how she'd taken great care to hide it all behind a gruff exterior and unreachable expectations. Of how only when everything all spilled open inadvertently and created a lot of distrust between her and her children and grandchildren and even with her husband . . . Lovina realized that she, too, had once thought she was stuck. That change wasn't possible.

She'd assumed her only option was to cover up the past. To keep secrets even from those you loved best.

She'd been wrong, of course.

"You are old enough to make your own decisions," Lovina said quietly. "And though most who know me would be somewhat surprised to hear me say this, I'll tell you that you should make your decisions about your future on your own."

Her lips slightly parted, Annie stared at Lovina in wonder. At last she nodded her understanding.

Lovina smiled back. And because they seemed to have reached an agreement of sorts, she said, "Sometimes, I think life is like the ground in winter."

Annie's eyebrows lifted. "How so?"

"Sometimes we only see the brown earth, with the fields looking dried up and ugly. It seems that we'll never see anything beautiful again. We wish with all our might for a good snow to fall. For everything to be covered up. Then, everything would be beautiful, covered by a bright, glistening layer of perfection."

Annie nodded, urging her to continue.

"But what I've learned—and what you might want to think about, dear—is that eventually, the snow always melts."

"And underneath?" Annie whispered.

"And underneath, one will find one of two things: Either everything will be the same as it ever was, no better, no worse. Or, sometimes, one finds that everything has been cleansed." She smiled softly. "And then, every once in a while, the Lord gives us special gift."

"What?"

"A lovely, fresh, bright green blade of new grass." Just thinking of that sign of spring, Lovina smiled. "He reminds us that while the snow might come . . . it always melts. And in its place can be something truly lovely."

Annie leaned forward. "Lovina, have you ever seen such a thing?"

"Something beautiful where there was once nothing?" She smiled, then gave in to her impulse and curled her hand around Annie's. "All the time, dear. All the time."

Chapter 12

We don't know yet if dogs get the chicken pox. So far? Frank is not itchy.

Gregory, Age 7

Maybe it had been a big mistake to think she could host this year's Christmas dinner.

That thought had been spinning in Elsie's head all morning. Ever since Amanda and Viola had walked into her kitchen two hours ago. They'd arrived with pads of paper, a handful of pencils, and all sorts of great ideas.

As she heard those ideas, Elsie's confidence began to falter a bit. She'd wanted to host this dinner to prove to both herself and her family that she was just as capable as everyone else.

But now she was starting to get the feeling that she'd been fooling herself. "Nineteen people for dinner is rather more than I had imagined."

"It is," Viola agreed, "but we can handle it. We three girls can handle just about anything together."

"I'm not so sure about that."

Amanda placed her warm palm on Elsie's hand. "It could be worse, I suppose. Your uncle Aden was going to come out this way but the weather is supposed to turn."

"Really?" Elsie asked. It had been the driest winter that any of them could recall.

"I, for one, hope the weather does turn. I'd love for Annie to experience a white Christmas," Viola said.

Elsie hadn't been able to spend much time with the girl yet. "How's she getting along with Mommi?"

"I think she really likes living with our grandparents. They seem to have mastered spending time with her and not being too intrusive."

Elsie shook her head in wonder. "I love Mommi, you both know that. But I've never considered spending time with her to be particularly easy."

Amanda chuckled. "I think they've mellowed a bit over the years. Regina loves being with them, too. Whenever I need a babysitter, she asks to be with her Lovina."

Elsie sighed. "I suppose if Annie can come all the way over here from Belize and stay with Mommi and Dawdi, I'll have to get over my nerves."

Amanda squeezed her hand again. "Elsie, both Roman and I were so happy that you wanted to host Christmas dinner. I was honored that you asked me to help. I promise, everything will get done and it will be perfect."

Viola chuckled. "Amanda, you are too sweet. I can practically promise our meal won't be perfect, but we will all be together. That's all that matters to me."

At last, Elsie relaxed. Her twin was exactly right. Dinner didn't have to be perfect or fancy. All it needed was their loved ones, and they had that in spades.

Getting to her feet, she reached down to pat Betsy, who stood up as well. "In that case, let's call Lorene and see what she wants to bring. And then tell our husbands to go to Daybreak and borrow the card tables and chairs that Atle said we could use. We've got plenty to do."

When Ruth got back to her apartment after another long day at the Rhodeses' *haus*, she looked at the pretty pink quilt, the perfectly aligned books, the neatly put-away dishes and glasses. The kitchen sink was clean and empty; the bathroom countertop practically sparkled. Everything was fresh and clean and neat.

It was exactly the living space that she'd always dreamed of having.

It was also the perfectly wrong place for her at the moment.

And she realized she couldn't be there another second. She needed another person to talk to, not peace and quiet. She needed some advice, not time for reflection.

Before she changed her mind, she turned on her heel and rushed down the sidewalk to Daybreak. If she was lucky, Kristy would still be on her shift or just coming off of it.

After saying hello to Florence and some of the other staff members, she discovered that her hunch was correct. Kristy had just finished her shift and was in the staff room gathering her things together.

And luckily, she was also very happy to see Ruth. "Long time no see," she teased. "I thought you were going to keep me informed about how your job was going."

"I had planned on it, but I've been busier than I ever imagined."

Kristy looked at her again, this time a little bit more closely. Then she smiled wider. "I don't know what's happened, but you seem happier."

Well, now. That was a shock. "I don't know if I am happier. But I definitely have some things to share. That is, if you have time to chat."

"I do." Glancing up at the clock on the wall, she said, "Floyd is going to pick me up in about an hour. I was going to work on my knitting while I waited. Now we can chat."

Ruth didn't need a second invitation. "Want some hot chocolate?"

"Of course. You get the hot chocolate and I'll get the cookies. The cook made some really delicious peppermint-bark cookies. I'll meet you here in five minutes."

Five minutes later, they were eating chocolate brownie cookies decorated with crushed peppermint candy and sipping hot chocolate.

While they indulged in their chocolate snack, Ruth relayed everything she could about Martin and his kids. She finished her story by describing the latest news, filling Kristy in on Gregory's case of probable chicken pox and Martin's sudden invitation.

Through it all, Kristy was the perfect listener. But when Ruth finished her summary, her eyes got wide. "Oh, Ruth. Only you would get talked into being in such a home."

Wondering if maybe she'd been laying things on a little too thick, Ruth winced. "It's not a bad place, Kristy. Simply disorganized and hectic."

"I'm surprised he asked you to move in with them."

"It did take me off guard. So much so, I didn't know what to say at first."

"I wouldn't have known what to say, either."

"At first I feared he was joking. I mean, it's not like he doesn't have any extended family. There would have to be someone better than me, right?"

"Maybe."

"Maybe? I thought you would be as shocked as me."

"I am. But I also can't say that I blame him for wanting you there," Kristy murmured as she looked at Ruth over the rim of her mug. "You are exceptionally calm and stalwart in a crisis. And it's obvious he is worried about his son. Why wouldn't he want your help?"

Ruth shifted uncomfortably under her girlfriend's gaze. "I don't mind helping him. I want to help him. I'm worried about Gregory, too. And worried that the other *kinner* are all going to get sick, too."

"Then what is the problem?"

Thinking about that, she shrugged. "It's a lot of things. It's the way he seems to have forgotten that I have a life outside of his house. He shouldn't expect me to drop everything in order to take care of his sick children twenty-four hours a day. Especially not at Christmas," she added, hoping against hope that she sounded as if she did, indeed, have other things to do.

She wished she did.

"That does seem rather presumptuous of him."

"I'll say. Because it is."

"So you're going to say no? Just let him deal with his *kinner* on his own?"

Put that way, it did sound pretty harsh. Of course, more to the point, she hadn't actually decided that she was going to refuse to help him. "I'm not sure."

"Really?" Kristy's voice was more bemused than upset. And her expression was a mixture of surprise and something far more calculating. Almost as if she knew about a secret plan that Ruth didn't. "So you actually are considering moving in to help with the children over Christmas."

"If all the *kinner* get chicken pox, I'm afraid I might have to."

"Oh, Ruth."

"Honestly, you don't know what they're like. They're beyond handfuls. Why, why . . . they are worse than a basketful of kittens when they're all happy and healthy. Thinking of all six of them cranky and itchy at the same time? It's frightening to imagine."

"But Ruth—"

Ruth exhaled, looked at her best friend in Sugarcreek, and decided to take a leap of faith. "The truth is that I'm afraid I would really regret not helping out Martin and his children. They need me. And, well, this is going to sound hard to imagine, but I think I need them."

Kristy's expression softened. She reached out to grab Ruth's hand. "Oh, Ruth. I know this is a hard time of the year for you. But you can always spend time with my family. We'd love to have you."

But that was the point, Ruth knew. If she spent the holidays with Kristy and her family, she would once again be the visitor, the outsider looking in. And, well, she'd done that. She'd done that a lot.

At the Rhodeses' house, she was becoming a part of them. Oh, not really. She of course realized that she wasn't actually a member of the family. She was only a paid employee. But because those *kinner* were so needy, because Martin seemed to appreciate every little thing she did, even when she didn't do it very well—it made her feel needed.

"Kristy, I've spent most of my life trying to be grateful for any attention. I made due with less affection, less time, less things. Less everything."

"Oh, Ruth—"

She held up a hand. "I'm sorry. I know I sound sorry for myself. Pitiful, even. But that's not how I'm trying to be. It's just that it's been hard, and I fear that I'm in this place where I am now because of all those experiences."

"Anyone would feel that way," Kristy pointed out.

Ruth wondered if that was true. Her childhood had been less than ideal. But she also realized that she wasn't the only grown woman to have to deal with some painful memories.

"Now, after spending time with the Rhodes family, I feel a bit like one of Martin's Christmas trees. I'm sturdy and just fine on my own. But if I was mixed in with some festive decorations and maybe even covered with lights, I would glow with happiness."

Kristy frowned. "Ruth, you already are special. You don't need anything more to be worthy."

"I'm not trying to be worthy, Kristy. I just want to surround myself with a little bit of brightness and merriment. Soon enough, I'll go back to my regular life. I'll go back to being plain old Ruth. But right now God has given me an opportunity to be an actual part of a family this Christmas. They aren't asking me to stay with them because they feel obligated or out of pity. They need me."

"They need you to cook and clean and nurse them through chicken pox."

"I know that. However, they also need me to read stories and hold their hands and make cards and games. They need to have a merry Christmas in spite of their being sick, their father being overworked, and their mother being gone to heaven." She lowered her voice. "But what they don't realize is that I need to be around those *kinner* and Martin even more. I feel that they might not realize it but the Lord does, and He's given me this opportunity."

Kristy's eyes looked suspiciously damp. "You need to do what your heart tells you to do. And what you feel the Lord is wanting you to do, too."

Ruth was so glad Kristy had mentioned the Lord's will. She really did believe that He had to have been guiding them all together. Why else would she have crossed paths with Lovina Keim on the exact day that she'd received notice about her job?

Why else would she feel so at ease around the children when everyone knew they were a handful?

And why else would Ruth—who always kept to herself—even be considering such a thing as moving in with a man and his kids to help out over Christmas? These feelings of openness and happiness, they had to be a gift from God.

He'd been a fool. A scared and frightened one at that.

Why else would he have asked Ruth to move in with them? The moment he'd thrown out his idea, he could practically feel her shock.

And why wouldn't she be shocked? She was

a young woman doing him a favor. Of course she would have dozens of other things to do besides help him nurse his children.

But boy, did he wish he wasn't sitting alone at the moment.

Actually, he wasn't exactly alone. He was sitting next to Gregory, who was restlessly sleeping. Across the room, his brother Thomas was sound asleep, never moving or twitching, as was his way. Thomas was as solid a sleeper as he was a busy child. He'd always been that way, too. Even as a baby he'd slept through the night, and Grace had used to press her palm to his chest to make sure it was moving, declaring that she simply couldn't understand how such a busy boy could sleep so soundly.

Gregory, on the other hand, had been the complete opposite. He'd been far more easygoing during his waking hours, but hated to sleep.

At the moment, the pain reliever seemed to be doing some good. His fever had lessened and he'd been asleep for a solid two hours.

Getting to his feet, Martin straightened the sheets around the boy, did the same for Thomas, then quietly walked into the hall.

And was brought up short by the sight of Brigit sitting on the floor of the hallway, Frank curled by her side.

"Hi," she said.

"Hi to you, too." Since he was too tired to take her downstairs, he elected to do the easiest thing and simply sit next to her on the floor. "Any special reason you're up?"

She stretched her toes. "Nope. I was up, then I got thirsty. Then I decided to wait for you with Frank."

"I'm glad Frank was keeping you company."

"Me, too. He's a *gut* dog."

"He is. When he's asleep."

Brigit's lips curved up as she gently petted the dog. After smoothing her little hand over the golden fur a couple of times she glanced up at him. "Are you worried about Gregory?"

"Well, I'm worried about him because I don't want him to be feverish or uncomfortable. But I'm not worried about chicken pox. Most people get it one time or another."

"Did you get it?"

"Yep. When I was just about your age."

"Did Mamm?"

"You know what? I'm sure she did, but I don't remember us ever discussing chicken pox."

"What about Ruth? Did she have chicken pox?"

"Yes, she did."

"That's *gut*. Now she won't get sick."

"That is *gut*." Looking down at his sweet little girl, he asked, "Brigit, are you worried about getting sick?"

"Kind of."

"Are you worried about being sick at Christmas?"

"Kind of. But if Gregory is gonna be all right, I guess I'll be all right, too."

Martin chuckled. "That's the way to think, dear. It's always best to try to be positive." Of course, as soon as he said those words he was wishing that he'd been a bit more positive lately.

"Daed, I'm glad Ruth is taking care of us. She's real nice."

"*Jah*, she is." Actually, he thought she was pretty special.

"Do you think she likes us?"

"I hope so. That is, I hope we don't drive her too crazy," he teased. "There are a lot of us, you know."

Brigit nodded, then blurted, "She told me something today."

She looked so solemn and earnest, he leaned in closer to her and Frank. "What was that?"

"She said that she didn't grow up in just one house. That she had to live in a whole lot of houses because her parents died."

"I knew she had a difficult time of it, but that is mighty sad."

She leaned into his side and sighed. "I think so, too."

Martin wrapped an arm around her shoulders. "We can't do anything about her past, but we can

all do something about the present, don'tcha think? We'll have to make this a happy Christmas for Ruth."

Brigit's smile was radiant as she scrambled to her feet. "I'm gonna go tell that to Karin."

"I think that's a fine idea, dear. But wait until the morning when she's awake. If you let Karin know, she'll make sure everyone does what they are supposed to do."

After she scampered up the stairs, Martin stretched out on the floor next to their puppy. When Frank cuddled closer, Martin closed his eyes and let himself relax.

And then remembered to give thanks for his blessings, those great and small.

Chapter 13

*Katrina really doesn't like to be teased about
getting red spots on her face.*

Karin, Age 5

Most of Ruth's earliest childhood memories existed
in her head as a hazy blur, interrupted only by stark
moments of happiness or extreme sadness.

She didn't need a counselor to help her understand
why she'd blocked most memories out. That had
been her way to cope with all the confusion she'd
felt as a little girl. It had been difficult to understand
why she'd never been especially wanted by her relatives. She hadn't understood why God had decided
that He'd needed her parents at such a young age.
And especially when they'd had a little girl to take
care of.

She'd also learned that understanding why anything happened didn't necessarily make things easier. Sometimes all that was necessary was making do.

And so that was what she'd learned to do. She'd learned to live in the moment. She'd learned not to think about her future, and she'd learned not to dwell on the past. Instead, she'd focused on the present.

But that morning, she'd woken up with a memory so stark and vivid she would have sworn that it had happened just hours ago, not six years.

It had been when she'd been fourteen, gangly, and awkward. Shy and secretly angry, she'd been spending a year living with her mother's youngest sister, Rachel, and Josiah, her husband of two years. Rachel had been pregnant and had been expecting their baby right around Christmas. She'd fairly glowed with happiness, and her husband had been particularly doting and kind.

Every morning Josiah would make them breakfast and fuss over Rachel like she was the first woman in Charm to be pregnant.

Ruth had understood why Josiah had loved her so much. Rachel was one of the nicest people Ruth had ever known. From the moment Ruth had moved in, Rachel had gone out of her way to make her feel welcome. In return, some of Ruth's anger had melted away and she'd begun doing everything she could to make a good impression. She'd cooked supper, done laundry, gathered eggs, shoveled snow. Anything she could do to make Rachel's life easier. For them to want to keep her longer.

Over and over both Josiah and Rachel told her that she was a blessing to them. That they didn't know what they would have done without her. Never having received such praise, Ruth had practically eaten it up.

Then, three days before Christmas, Rachel had her baby girl. They'd named her Hope, and Hope was lovely and perfect. Ruth was looking forward to helping out, to holding baby Hope whenever Rachel needed her rest, to helping make that Christmas especially *wunderbaar*.

But on the morning of Christmas Eve, another relative stopped by. Evan and his wife, Francis, who were Josiah's aunt and uncle. They both were thin and wiry, stern looking and strict. Ruth had stayed out of their way, keeping to her room and working on the blanket she was crocheting for Hope.

And that was why she'd been so shocked when Josiah had entered her room and told her to get her things together.

"But why?" she'd asked. "What did I do wrong?"

"Not a thing. But we only agreed to keep you until the baby came." Looking slightly guilty, he simply stated, "And the baby came."

"Where am I going to stay now?"

"With my aunt and uncle." A shadow entered his

eyes before he visibly brushed it to one side. "They agreed to take you in for six months."

"I have to go with Evan and Francis?"

"*Jah.*"

"But—"

He lowered his voice. "They're kind of strict, but they should treat you okay. And there's nothing I can do. I mean, I did what I promised, right?"

Feeling desolate, she nodded. She didn't want to upset Josiah further. He'd been so good to her. Until now. "I'll be ready in a few minutes."

Looking a bit guilty, he pressed his hand on her shoulder. "Ruth?"

"Yes?" She looked into his eyes, waiting for something. A promise. Anything.

He gestured to the blanket. "Rachel said you could take your project with you."

"Oh. All right." They hadn't wanted her gift to them. They hadn't wanted anything.

Knowing that the blanket would always serve as a reminder of yet another unsuccessful attempt to belong, she left it behind. And when she rode in the buggy beside Evan and Francis, watching the one place she'd felt comfortable drift away, she knew that there wouldn't be any Christmas gifts waiting for her at their house.

She hadn't been wrong.

Now, in the morning light of her small one-room apartment, with its pink walls and pretty quilt, Ruth made a decision. She was going to pull out her tote bag, pack her things, and prepare to spend the next two or three weeks taking care of the Rhodes *kinner*.

No matter what, she didn't want any of them to ever imagine that they were unwanted. Or a burden. Especially not if she could help it. Especially not on Christmas.

With that in mind, Ruth gathered more things than she thought she would need, carefully carried them all downstairs, and accepted her landlady's neighbor's offer of help.

She was going to the Rhodeses' house for as long as they needed her. Because even if it was hectic and tiring and full of sick, crying kids and too many cases of chicken pox, it was sure to be a far sight better than the Christmas of her fourteenth year.

The year she'd realized that nothing was ever going to change. And that it was completely possible for things to get even worse than she'd imagined.

When Larry, the neighbor, pulled up in front of the Rhodeses' house, Ruth thought it had never looked so quiet. Here it was, already eight in the morning and no lights were shining, shades were pulled down, and the barn looked quiet, too.

"You sure someone's here, Ruth?" Larry asked. "It looks pretty quiet."

"Six children under ten live here, along with one fluffy dog with an enormous tail," she said dryly. "I don't think Martin takes any of them anywhere if he can help it."

Larry chuckled. "I think you might have a point." After unbuckling his seat belt, he turned to her. "Just the same, I'm going to help you get your things inside and make sure this is where you want to be. No way am I going to leave here without your being settled."

His words were so sweet—so opposite the way so many of her relatives had treated her—tears pricked her eyes. But because, of course, he wouldn't understand her sudden burst of emotion, she simply nodded and scrambled out her side of the car.

Then she met him at the hatchback and grabbed one of her three bags. Larry took the other two and followed her to the front door, where she set down her bag and knocked.

And then knocked again.

Larry looked through the window, leaned back, and shrugged. "I don't know, Ruth. It doesn't seem as if anyone—"

Just then, the door burst opened and Thomas

poked his head out. "Ruth! You came!" he chirped. "Boy, am I happy to see ya!"

There it went again! Her eyes pricked with unshed tears. "Thomas, I am happy to see you, too. Where is everyone?"

"Sick."

"Sick? Oh, my." Ruth looked at her driver. "I think I better go in and start taking care of things right now."

Larry grabbed the handles of her bags. "Let me help you get these inside. Young man, hold open the door."

Thomas complied, his gaze focused on Ruth's suitcases. "You moving in, Ruth?"

Larry looked at her curiously.

"*Jah*. Your father asked me to stay here and look after you since Gregory is sick."

"But he didn't think you were gonna say yes."

"I guess he'll be surprised, then." Aware that Larry was standing stock-still in the middle of the entryway, obviously in no hurry to drop her things and run, Ruth attempted to smile. "Thank you again, Larry." Remembering that the Rhodes were New Order and had a phone in their kitchen, she added, "I'll call you in a day or so and let you know when I am returning."

"I'm not as worried about your coming back as I am about your staying here with a houseful of sick kids."

"I'll be okay."

"Are you sure? It don't feel right, leaving you like this. I feel like I'm leaving you to the wolves."

Where had a man like him been when she was younger? "I appreciate your concern. More than you know. But I think I better see where everyone else is."

Larry nodded. "All right then." Reaching out, he clasped her hand and squeezed gently, his wrinkled hand with the paper-soft skin over a map of veins, bringing more comfort than he would ever realize. "Call us tonight, though. Okay? Otherwise the Mrs. and I are gonna worry."

"I'll call." She kept her smile on her face until he turned, left the house, and disappeared from view.

Actually, the smile wasn't hard to keep in place because Thomas had edged closer and slid his hand into hers. That little gesture made her feel even more wanted and squeezed her heart just a little bit more.

After closing the door, she knelt down in front of him so they were eye level. "Thomas, you are in pajamas."

"I know."

"Where's your father?"

"Holding Meg." He tucked in his bottom lip and chewed on it. "She's sick now, too. And so is Karin."

"Oh, boy. I think I better go see how I can help, hmm?"

"Yeah." He grabbed her hand again and pulled her

forward. Only to stop on the second step. Then he looked up at her, his expression fierce and earnest. "You promise you're going to stay, Ruth?"

"I promise. I promise I will stay as long as you want me."

He still looked doubtful. "You *promise* you promise?"

She took care to keep her own expression just as earnest. "*Jah*, Thomas. I promise to keep my promise."

Then, to her surprise, he smiled, too. A big smile. The kind of smile most people smiled on their birthdays. Or on Christmas. Or when they got a new puppy. "*Gut*," he muttered as he let go of her hand and raced upstairs.

Ruth followed far more slowly, but realized that for once, she'd just made a promise that she had every intention of keeping.

Because at the moment it felt like the best promise she'd ever made.

Chapter 14

Kittens make everything better.

Meg, Age 4

Life with Annie was proving to be one of the most gratifying experiences of Lovina's life. She was learning new things, too!

And at her age! And after raising six children and watching many of her grandchildren grow up and get married.

It just went to show you that the Lord was full of surprises. Always.

She was thinking about such things as she was making a pot of chili. She'd needed something to do when Annie had opted to join Elsie, Roman, and their spouses on their trip into town for some last-minute Christmas shopping, then for lunch at the Farmstead.

Funny how one very quiet girl could make such a difference in her life. Now when she was gone, Lovina felt a little bit of a loss about what to do with herself.

Two raps on the door interrupted her thoughts. "Come in, Viola," she called out, thinking that she was glad Viola had something of a signature knock.

And sure enough, in came pretty Viola, who happened to be practically glowing in good health. "Look at you," Lovina teased. "You are all smiles today. Is it because you girls have got everything in hand for our Christmas dinner?"

"We don't quite have everything in hand, but we're almost there."

"That's *gut*. Because, you know, tomorrow is Christmas Eve."

"We'll do it. I promise."

"I know you will, dear," Lovina said. "I'm proud of you. Proud of both of my dear twin granddaughters."

Viola's eyes shone. "Oh, Mommi. Elsie and I have really been enjoying ourselves. I've missed my twin. And Mommi, you should see Elsie. She is so happy to have something important to do."

Lovina inwardly winced. "We should have known better than to hover as much as we have. Everyone needs to feel needed." Which, she decided, was what hosting Annie had done for her. She really felt like Annie needed their conversations and projects. And that, of course, made Lovina want to do even more with her.

Viola walked to the pot of chili, took a sniff, and smiled. "Is it ready yet?"

"Not yet. Plus, I still need to make some corn bread to go with it."

"I could do that."

"I know you could. But I'd rather you simply talk to me. What's on your mind, dear?"

"Annie."

"I thought maybe so. Is everything all right with her?"

Viola studied her closely. So closely that Lovina could practically see her granddaughter's mind spinning.

And that made her a bit nervous, not that she would ever let Viola know that. "Is she upset about something?"

Viola leaned back against one of the counters. "I don't know. Mommi, I really don't know Annie all that well. As I told you and Dawdi, her father kept her out of the mission for the most part. He's a dedicated servant to the Lord."

"I've heard that."

Viola swallowed. "I'm embarrassed to say I didn't give her all that much thought. Edward keeps a busy schedule, and I've had my hands full trying to be as good a helpmate as I can be."

"That's a good thing, child."

"I thought so, but now . . . Mommi, Annie looks like a different person here."

"Surely not. She hasn't been here that long."

"But you've made a difference to her."

"I'm happy to hear that."

"I spoke with her this morning. She confided how you told her about snow. About how it covered things up that weren't pretty but only for a short time." Again, Viola gave her grandmother a curious look.

And again, Lovina felt a little awkward. "Viola, I can't help but speak my mind."

"I'm glad you did. When she and I talked this morning, Annie told me that she was actually thinking about her life for the very first time. Because you made her realize that she has choices." She shook her head in wonder. "You've done something remarkable, Mommi."

"Not at all. If anything special happened, it was because of Annie herself. And, of course, the Lord working through her."

Viola grinned, startling Lovina so much that she stopped grating the block of cheddar cheese and glared for good measure. "What is that grin for?"

"Because though you always speak your mind, you don't usually take such care with your words."

"I wouldn't say that."

"I would, and so would everyone else. Usually,

you speak your mind with such force and confidence that a bulldozer wouldn't interfere with your will."

"That's a bit of an exaggeration."

"If it is, it's only a small one," she said around a smile. Wrapping her arms around Lovina's waist, she leaned close and rested her head on Lovina's back. "Mommi, I came in here to tell you thank you. To tell you that you proved me right, and I wasn't even sure I was right. Thanks for letting Annie stay with you and Dawdi so I could spend some time with Elsie. You're making this Christmas really special for her."

Such compliments embarrassed Lovina. And were so out of the ordinary, they made Lovina feel uncomfortable, too.

And so, because of that, she brushed them off. "She's here because of you and your husband, Viola. I think that means you've had quite a part in making the holiday special for her, too."

"Yes, but—"

"If you're going to start sprinkling around compliments like birdseed, then you should take your fair share of them, too."

Viola buttoned her lips, but her eyes were twinkling. "*Jah*, Mommi."

"Let's not discuss this again," Lovina said brusquely. "I don't want anyone to feel like they're being talked about."

"All right, Mommi."

Then, because Lovina was feeling warm and cozy, and loved and secretly almost as happy as Viola looked, she reached down, took out a box of corn bread mix, and turned to face Viola. "Now, because you offered, you may make some corn bread. Unless you don't feel like helping me out any longer."

"I'll make the corn bread, Mommi. I'll be happy to."

"*Danke*, dear." Then, because she couldn't help it, Lovina leaned down and pressed her lips to Viola's forehead. "You are a *wonderful-gut* girl, Viola. And if I may say so, you've turned into a *wonderful-gut* woman."

"*Danke*, Mommi."

For the last ten minutes, Martin had been pinned under a cranky, crying four-year-old on the edge of a narrow, unmade twin bed.

It was not comfortable.

And because he had six *kinner*, the situation wasn't something he was totally unfamiliar with. He had dealt with his fair share of tired and sick children over the years. He'd learned to take things minute by minute instead of worrying about everything he couldn't control.

He'd also learned to pray. Prayer always helped.

Unfortunately, at the moment his neck was getting a crick in it from his awkward position, and he didn't feel quite right asking the Lord to alleviate his pain.

Instead, he attempted to think of the positive, just like Ruth seemed to be so fond of doing. With that in mind, he gave thanks that he was currently lying down next to Meg and not carrying her around the house. And that the worst of her crying jag seemed to have ended.

Once the muscles in his shoulders eased, he allowed himself to close his eyes. And suddenly, he was too comfortable to get up when he heard Thomas answer the door to Ruth, who came in with some man, then close the door.

Relief poured through him when he heard Ruth's pleasant voice drift up the stairs. She'd come back.

Thank you, Got, he murmured.

"Daed, who's there?" Meg asked in a sleepy voice.

"Sounds like Ruth and maybe a driver. Thomas let her in."

Meg waited a beat. Then another one. Then exhaled around a hiccup. "Oh."

"*Jah*, oh," he murmured under his breath.

Now it was an even better idea to get up and see to things. He couldn't have Meg seeing him ignore Ruth.

And he would get up. In just a few minutes. Hopefully.

Instead, he kept his face turned toward the door as he heard their slow progression up the stairs.

"What's going on?" Meg whispered.

"I don't know because I'm here with you. I should probably move, don't ya think?"

After the smallest of pauses, she shook her head. "Not yet."

Now that she'd shifted and wasn't crying anymore, and he'd stopped worrying so much and had finally relaxed, he was almost comfortable. With that in mind, he gave her a little squeeze. "I'll stay here a little longer."

"Promise?"

"Promise."

She sighed.

Voices drifted up. It sounded as if Ruth had a good number of suitcases. Then it sounded as if Katrina and Brigit were talking to her.

It really was time to get up. He'd just moved Meg when Ruth at last appeared, poking her head into the room, her bright blue eyes blinking in confusion, then humor, when she spied him lazing about on the bed. "Martin, are you sick, too?"

"*Nee.* There's a story here, but I'll save it for another day." Grinning at her, he got to his feet. "It sounds as if you brought a couple of suitcases with ya?"

"I did." She looked down at her feet, which at the moment were only covered in thick tights covered with black-and-gold-striped socks. "I decided to accept your offer."

At last, it was official. Breathing a sigh of relief, he murmured, "I'm mighty glad that you decided to come back. I feared that I'd scared you off."

"You didn't." She tilted her head to one side, obviously taking in Meg's prone form and his ragged appearance. "But maybe I should've been more scared." As she walked toward them, her steps became more pronounced. "Meg, what is wrong with you?"

"I think I got the pox."

"I'm pretty sure she does," Martin said. "She's got the same symptoms Gregory has."

Meg rubbed her right eye with the side of one hand. "I'm icky."

Ruth gazed at Meg, taking in the little girl's tear-stained cheeks, flushed color, ratty hair, and running nose in one fell swoop. Then, to Martin's amazement, she threw her head back and laughed.

"Indeed you are. You're an icky mess, for sure and for certain."

"I don't wanna be a mess."

When Meg's bottom lip started to quiver, Ruth sat down next to her, neatly forcing Martin to climb off the bed and get to his feet. "Meg, it's time you stopped crying," she said. "No good ever comes of tears, and it usually makes things a fair bit worse."

"But—"

"No buts, child." Curving herself around Meg, Ruth neatly pulled a tissue out of the box on the bedside table and held it up to Meg's nose. "Now, blow."

To Martin's amazement, Meg did just that. Without complaining. Without whining. Without adding one more teardrop.

Standing in the doorway, Martin murmured, "Ruth, we are obliged." When he noticed that Thomas was standing just outside in the hallway, he put a hand on the boy's shoulder and gave him a reassuring squeeze. Right away Thomas relaxed against him. "You are a miracle worker."

Ruth glanced his way and winked. "Not so much. I'm new, that's all."

No, he was fairly sure that her newness had nothing to do with it. The fact was that she was competent. Capable and productive. "I am *verra* glad you decided to return."

"Me, too."

"Me, three," Thomas said. "Especially because she promised she'd stay for as long as we needed her," he added with a smile.

"Hopefully not too much past Christmas," she murmured.

"To be sure," Martin murmured. But inside his heart, he was thinking that her staying longer wouldn't be such a bad thing at all.

"Ruth, I'll go put your bags in the study downstairs. The couch in there folds down into a bed. I was thinking that maybe that might be a better spot for you instead of one of the children's bedrooms. The study has a door, so you'll have some peace and quiet at night. And it's a bit apart so you'll have some privacy, too. I hope that will be okay with you?"

She blinked. "*Jah*. I think it will be just fine, Martin. Now, I know you need to head to work. Go on. I'll see to my things after I sit with Meg for a bit."

"*Jah*, I guess I should head over to the farm to see how Floyd is doing without me." Turning to his son, he said, "Thomas, let's go see how the rest of the household is doing. And go get some sheets for Ruth's bed."

"Okay, Daed. But I gotta warn you. The rest of the kids don't look good."

He stilled. "Oh?"

"Katrina's sick and Karin just threw up. And so did Frank. I hate to say it, Daed, but at the moment, I'm the best you got."

"Ruth, I think I'll stick around here a little longer," he called out as he went to check up on Katrina and Karin.

Thomas grinned as he led the way back downstairs with Martin following. Now not regretting his decision to lie down with Meg for those brief scant minutes.

It was looking plenty certain that he wasn't going to have another moment like that for a long time.

Chapter 15

*Those ghosts that visit Scrooge seem kind of mean
to me. I, for one, wouldn't do a thing they said.*

Thomas, Age 8

The moment Martin and Thomas disappeared from
sight, Meg tugged on the sleeve of Ruth's dress. "Are
you really going to stay?"

"I am."

"For a long time?"

"I'll be here until all of you *kinner* are feeling
better. At least a couple of more days."

"But then?"

"But then I'll go back home, dear," she said lightly.

"But what if we don't get better by Christmas?"

Since Christmas was in two days, Ruth was pretty
sure they weren't going to be better by then. "If you're
not, it will still be Christmas, and Christmas is about

Jesus' birth, ain't so?" When Meg nodded solemnly, she added, "I promise I'll stay until all of you do feel better, but I don't think you're going to have to worry about that. I promise, you're itchy and uncomfortable now, but the worst of it will pass soon."

"Sure?"

"I am sure. The chicken pox is no fun, but it always fades away. And then all you're left with is the memory." She held out her hand. "Let's go get your face washed. Then we'll straighten up your bed. Why, it looks like wild animals got ahold of your bed and rumpled all of your sheets. Did that happen last night?"

Meg's lopsided smile returned. *"Nee."*

"Are you sure?"

"I'm sure," she said, this time with a giggle. "No animals were in my bed last night. At least, I don't think so!"

Ruth shook her head in mock worry as she guided Meg out of bed, slipped her robe around her, and walked her to the bathroom. "It seems I better be on the lookout for roving animals in the night."

"Ruth, there's only Frank here, and he sleeps in the kitchen."

"Hmm."

She turned on the faucet, let the water run until it got warm, then carefully bathed Meg's face and neck. Afterward, she brushed out the girl's hair and braided it neatly. By the time she had finished, Meg was yawning.

Leaving the child there to brush her teeth, Ruth returned to the room and straightened the bed, feeling almost like a mother. Funny, growing up, she'd always wished for someone to look after her. But at the moment she was enjoying the feeling of fussing over a little girl.

"I'm back!" Meg said as she appeared at the door.

"And just in time, too. Off to bed you go." After tucking Meg under the covers, Ruth handed her her worn stuffed rabbit. "Close your eyes now, child. It's time to rest."

"Will you stay here with me?"

"I'm afraid I cannot. I need to check on your siblings."

"You sure?"

"I'm sure," Ruth said, now getting used to Meg's need to verify everything. "They are itchy and uncomfortable, too. Plus, your father needs to check on his trees. But don't worry, I'll be nearby. And I'll return soon. I promise."

Meg stared at her under the veil of half-closed lids. Then, finally, she nodded. " 'Kay."

"Okay, then."

After closing Meg's door, Ruth went downstairs. After assuring Martin that she would be fine for a few hours, she sent him on his way. Then she poured a couple of glasses of Sprite from the six-pack she'd brought with her, knowing how it helped upset stomachs. She then went back upstairs, strode down the hall, and started visiting with the girls and Gregory.

Of course they needed their beds straightened, too. Ruth quietly remade beds, listened to a myriad of complaints, took temperatures, and passed out pain reliever and glasses of the cold soda.

As she'd suspected, the rare treat went a long way toward soothing their ills.

Two hours later, she was sitting on the big brown couch in the hearth room, sipping orange-spiced tea—she'd brought that, too—and was thinking that she'd never felt so tired in her life.

Though she'd lit a fire, the room was still chilly. She pulled an afghan over her legs and let herself relax. In no time at all, she had her eyes closed, too.

She'd just entered that hazy place between sleep and alertness when she heard the kitchen door open and shut and the unmistakable sound of Martin striding her way.

Abruptly, she straightened and attempted to put herself to rights.

She wasn't quick enough. Martin appeared at the door just as she was folding the coverlet.

"Ruth, is everything all right?"

"Couldn't be better. I was just, um, taking a little break here on the couch."

His eyes skimmed over her as he approached, seeming to take in every wrinkle in her plum-colored dress and every strand of hair that was surely sticking out of her usually neat *kapp*. "You look tired."

"Just being lazy."

"Are you wanting to reconsider your decision to stay?"

She searched his face, half expecting to see a teasing glint in his eyes. But instead, he looked as serious as ever.

He was a man who was so weighed by burdens, it seemed as if he'd forgotten all about light conversation. That made her sad. Hoping to encourage a smile, she decided to tease him a bit. "Do you want me to answer you honestly?"

He blinked. But though he seemed confused by her question, he didn't look any lighter. "Of course."

"I am not reconsidering anything."

"I'm glad. I'm surprised, but I'm glad."

"You shouldn't be so surprised. No Christian woman would leave at a time like this."

"Oh. Of course."

Something flickered in his eyes, and with that, Ruth immediately regretted saying what she just had. It wasn't that she didn't mean that a Christian wouldn't offer help, but it had come across as vaguely sanctimonious.

Hoping to restore some of the good feelings between them, she raised a palm in the air and waved it a bit. "Actually, taking care of your *kinner* makes me feel like I'm being of use. It feels good to put these hands to use."

His brows rose. "You already were using them at Daybreak."

"*Jah*, but that's not the same."

"I think it—" He cut off his words as he abruptly reached out to her. Then, to her further surprise, he gently clasped one of her hands. "Ruth, you're bleeding."

"What? Where?" Actually, at the moment, she didn't feel much except for his touch or see anything except how different his hand looked from her own.

But then her voice died as he turned her hand so her fingernails were facing up. "Oh, Ruth. Look at you," he murmured.

With effort, she looked away from the way his fingers looked and directed her attention to her own.

And sure enough, the cold air, combined with all the hand-washing she'd been doing, had made some of the skin around her cuticles tear and bleed. Surely there couldn't be anything that looked less feminine. It also wasn't anything new. She had dry skin, and the harsh air of winter always made things worse.

"I'm sorry," she said. "I'll get up right now. I don't want to accidentally get blood on your couch."

"Don't be silly. You have to know that the couch is the least of my worries."

At the moment, she didn't know what to think. Worse, she wasn't sure what to do. Did she extricate her hand or let herself enjoy the simple feeling of being coddled?

As she sat there, dumbly staring at her hand grasped in his, he turned her hand in his, winced, then pulled a tissue from the box on the coffee table.

And then, to her further shock, gently dabbed at her skin. "Such tender skin, Ruth," he murmured.

She was embarrassed, and at the moment thanked the Lord that he wasn't looking at her face, because she feared it was probably ten shades of red. "My hands are rough," she whispered. "Not so tender."

"But underneath," he murmured, almost to himself. "Underneath, they're as fragile as a newborn's." Carefully, he folded her one hand in between both of his own. Immediately the warmth of his skin melted into hers, soothing the hurt. And for some reason, sending some of that warmth right through her body.

It had been a long time since she'd felt anyone's tender touch. So long that, she realized, she'd started to believe that her body was made only for work, never affection.

So long that she hardly even knew how to respond to such a caring gesture. "I'm surprised your hands aren't more rough," she blurted before she could think the better of it.

His head popped up. For the first time, his gaze met hers. "What?"

"I mean, you, uh, work outside all day with the trees. I would have thought that would have made your skin less smooth."

Now she was talking about the feel of his skin! Her embarrassment was almost complete.

But instead of dropping her hand like it was a hot potato, he simply looked bemused. "I wear leather gloves all day. It's necessary because of the bark and needles." His eyes lit up as he moved his hand and pressed it against hers, palm to palm. "Therefore, I guess you could say that mine are almost as tender as yours," he teased.

He was teasing her in a sweet way.

Right then and there, she became aware of two very important things:

One, her hands were, indeed, a symbol for the rest of her: Most people thought she was far tougher than she was, mainly because she took such pains to hide behind a tough exterior.

Second: She really, really liked having her hand encased in his. So much so that she hoped he didn't let her hand go anytime soon.

So much so that she hoped that when he did let go . . . he would find a reason to hold her hand again in the very near future.

It was a fairly tame wish, that was true.

But after a lifetime of being afraid to wish for anything, Ruth figured it was best, perhaps, to start small.

She was just staring at their hands, thinking about this new revelation when Thomas walked in, looked at them, and tilted his head to one side.

"Daed, why are you sitting on the couch holding Ruth's hand?"

Immediately, Ruth dropped her hands and jumped to her feet.

But Martin, on the other hand, merely leaned back against the cushions and looked coolly at his eldest boy. "Thomas, perhaps you could try speaking to me in a different tone of voice."

"But—"

"And you also might uncover your manners enough to greet Ruth."

Ruth blinked in surprise. Greet?

Thomas was obviously just as confused. "Greet Ruth? Why?"

Martin got to his feet and gazed down at Thomas. Right then and there, Martin seemed terribly tall and well-built. And Thomas seemed very, very small.

"Because she's been working herself half to death taking care of five cranky *kinner*," he murmured quietly. "Because she was willing to give up her own apartment, her own life, in order to cook our meals and wash our clothes. Because her fingers are bleeding. And because I told you to."

Thomas's eyes got big, he took a healthy step backward, and then he turned to Ruth. "Hello, Ruth." After darting an awkward glance at his father, Thomas thought for a moment, then sputtered, "Um, how are you?"

"I am well. *Danke.* And speaking of supper, I'm going to finish preparing it so you all can eat sooner rather than later. I'm sure you, Martin, are hungry after working outside all day."

She turned and darted into the kitchen, practically running to the sink. After running cool water over her hands, she washed them carefully, pulled out a few Band-Aids and patched up her fingers.

And then tried her very best to concentrate on making a salad and garlic bread to go with the lasagna she'd made an hour or so ago.

Anything would be better than to reflect on what had just happened in the hearth room.

Anything at all.

Chapter 16

Snow might make everything better but ice cream helps, too.

Brigit, Age 5

After Ruth had moved in, Martin divided his time between the farm and tending to all the *kinner*.

Yesterday, Floyd had hired another part-time worker to help in Martin's absence. Martin hated to spend some of their profits on another worker, but he also knew that there was nothing he could do about it. Customers were coming to the farm, and if they were going to keep them, they needed to be treated well. That meant that they needed to do everything they could to provide them the customer service they were used to receiving. But it still pinched.

He'd tried to help on the other end by doing some

of the accounting and finances late into the night at the dining room table.

That had turned out to be a mistake when Thomas had woken him up around midnight with the news that, he, too, had the chicken pox. His skin was flushed, he had a sizable blister on his side, and he was very concerned about correct protocol. Thomas, being Thomas, had stood in the hall for almost a half hour, debating whether to wake up Ruth—who was there to care for the sick children—or to wake up his father, because they were also supposed to treat Ruth like a guest, and one didn't wake up guests in the middle of the night when one had the chicken pox.

Thomas had relayed all of this until two that morning, crawling into bed with him, chattering, complaining, and basically demanding more attention than the other five children combined.

In light of this new circumstance—and the fact that Martin had slept through his alarm, which had gone off at four thirty that morning—Martin decided to stay home, hoping to keep his energy through sheer force of will.

That had been a mistake. It seemed that it was actually possible to drink three cups of coffee and still be dead on one's feet.

And as he had learned before Ruth had come to the rescue, being home was not easy.

It wasn't that he minded caring for six miserable, itchy, grumpy *kinner*. He didn't mind that—well not any more than the average person who was in such a situation, he assumed.

No, it was because he now was finding himself watching Ruth far too much.

He couldn't figure it out, but somehow everything she did interested him. He liked the tone of her voice, the melodic way it sounded when she read storybooks to the children. He liked her laugh. He liked how she never forgot to give particular attention to Frank, who was no doubt the hardest-working puppy in the county, being cradled, talked to, and fussed over by increasingly teary children.

And just when Martin was sure he'd convinced himself that there was nothing exceptionally special about Ruth, she did something that drew him to her like one of his children to the puppy.

Next thing he knew, he was chatting with her, helping her wash dishes, helping her carry laundry to the basement, delivering trays of soup and sandwiches as she made them.

To make matters worse, when he wasn't watching her and practically hanging on every smile or word she said, he was thinking about her.

Too much. He started thinking about her past. About why she didn't have any family. About what she usually did at Christmastime.

He found himself wondering if she'd been courted before. Every time he'd clumsily broached the subject she would change the topic.

Obviously, there was a story there. And though it was none of his business, he found himself wondering about what had happened.

And if, for some unknown reason, she hadn't been courted? Well, he wanted to know why she hadn't been. Had the men in her life been blind? Or had she held them off for a particular reason? He wished he knew.

He wished he knew everything about her. He was curious about her favorite books, flowers, pies, and season. It was all disconcerting, and all of it was none of his business, either.

But what was worse, he had a fairly good idea that she was starting to realize that he was becoming smitten.

Of course, she would have to be deaf, dumb, and blind not to notice his attention. Thomas had zeroed right in on Martin holding Ruth's hand, and Thomas was only eight.

By noon, Ruth was studying him, too.

Unfortunately, she wasn't gazing at him the way he was gazing at her. Instead, she kept darting curious glances at him, then would brush off a nonexistent crumb from her sleeve or shake her skirts, smoothing the fabric. That was when he realized that she didn't think he was staring at her because he couldn't seem to look away.

No, she thought he was staring at her because of some flaw.

And that was when he realized that Ruth had no feminine wiles. At all. She was a completely different sort than Grace, who had been sweet as could be, but also very aware of her pleasing appearance.

Grace had been pretty. She also had known it. He'd never thought that to be a bad thing, and he still didn't. It had given her a confidence around most people, and her lively nature had been a blessing when all of the *kinner* were so terribly small.

In addition, she'd accepted her beauty the way he'd accepted that he was taller than most and had broader shoulders. God had given them those attributes, and it would have been a shame to hide them.

But while Ruth might not have Grace's striking looks, she was far from being plain. Very far. She also had a quiet grace about her, and her easygoing nature was just as appealing as Grace's chatter and bright laughter.

But the difference was that Ruth had no idea she was so appealing. Actually, one would think she had a scar or a handicap or blemished skin or, well, something that someone had teased her about at one time or another.

Now, as he was sitting at the kitchen table watching her make a big pot of beef and barley soup, he knew he was in danger of saying something inappropriate. It wasn't the time to hint about his burgeoning feelings.

Martin shook his head. He needed to get some space.

"Ruth, I'm going to go to the tree farm."

She turned at his abrupt tone. Confusion—and, perhaps, disappointment—filled her features before she carefully tamped them down. "I didn't realize you were going in today."

"It can't be helped. It's almost Christmas, you know."

"Of course. Don't worry about your children. I'll take good care of them."

"I know you will," he said quietly before he realized that he was giving away too much. "I mean, you are doing a good job with the *kinner*. And they like you."

Warmth entered her eyes. "And I like them."

There was that pull again, tempting him to say more than he should. Tempting him to feel more than he'd ever felt before.

Carefully, he tamped it down again. It wouldn't do for her to know how much he'd started to think about her. "I won't be back until after supper."

"I'll save you a plate."

"That's not necessary."

"Maybe not. But still, I will save you a plate."

"*Danke.*" He turned, pushing away all the words that were on his tongue that had to do with all kinds of things that shouldn't be said. With more haste than was necessary, he grabbed his stocking cap, thick leather gloves, and wool coat, and exited, fastening his coat as he did so.

It was going to be a very long afternoon. He could only hope that he had so much work to do that he wouldn't have a spare minute to think about everything at home.

To settle on the person who had inadvertently made his house into a home, all over again.

Chapter 17

Daed says Christmas is for family. That's gut, 'cause we've got a lot of that.

Thomas, Age 8

The moment the door clicked tightly shut, Ruth leaned her head back and called herself every kind of a fool. "What did you think he was going to say to you, Ruth?" she murmured to herself. "That he was starting to feel something for you?"

Of course, she knew she was being more than a little harsh to both herself and Martin. They'd become friends, she knew that. She knew that even when she eventually left the Rhodeses' house and searched for a new job that she'd always be friends with Martin and his children.

She knew if they ran into each other in town or at the store they would probably stop and chat.

Being here was nothing, nothing like living in a relative's house, unwanted and as a focus of charity. She was getting paid for her time and getting paid well. She was also treated well, like an equal, and that was a nice thing.

She was the one who was at fault, suddenly changing their roles and wishing for things that couldn't happen. She was the one who was at fault, not him.

After checking on the children and seeing that Katrina and the twins were playing dolls in their room, Meg was napping, and Gregory was building a Lego set next to Frank, she realized that only Thomas was unaccounted for.

Happy to have something to do, Ruth walked up to his room and peeked in.

Sure enough, he was in his room, but not sleeping. Instead, he was lying on his side and staring out the window. When she entered the room, he rolled onto his other side and faced her. "Hiya, Ruth."

"Hiya to you, too," she replied with what she hoped was a cheerier smile than how she was feeling.

Sitting on the side of his bed, she reached out and felt his forehead and frowned. He was feverish and absolutely covered with spots. "You look like you've got a *gut* case of the pox," she murmured. "You might even have it the worst."

"Lucky me." He attempted to smile, but it faded almost immediately.

"Well, you do seem to take things to extremes, Thomas," she murmured as she reached out and lightly rubbed his back.

One corner of his lip rose before he frowned again. "I hate being sick."

"I know. In just a minute I'll go run you another oatmeal bath. Those seem to help."

"They make the water feel slimy and gross."

"I know. But what can you do?"

He stared at her for a minute before cracking a smile. "You're funny, Ruth."

"I'll take that as a compliment," she said lightly, though a lump had formed in her throat. She was really going to miss this little boy.

"*Nee*, I mean it," he said as his smile grew broader. "I like you being here. You make things better."

"I'm glad to hear that because I like being here."

"You do?"

"Of course I do, though I wish I was here for a different reason."

He blinked. "Like what kind of reason?"

Immediately, she wished she could rewind the last two minutes. "You know what I meant. I feel bad that all of you are sick, that's all. We could have had more fun together if everyone wasn't feeling so bad."

"When we're all better you'll be gone." He frowned.

She felt like frowning, too. But that wouldn't do, so she simply nodded. "*Jah*, I will, I'm afraid."

"I wish you were going to stay longer."

She did, too. "You *kinner* won't need me when you're back at school."

"Do you ever wish you were a part of our family? Then you could stay?"

What would be the benefit of admitting such a thing? "I wish a lot of things," she said evasively.

"Like what?"

Grasping at straws, she pointed to the window. "Well, I wish it would look more Christmasy. I wish it would snow."

"Me, too. Do you think we'll get snow for Christmas?"

When she noticed he was feeling a little chilled, she smoothed his covers and tucked him back in. "I don't know. I haven't been around anyone but you children. I'm not sure what the weather reports say."

"I hope it snows, but I doubt it will."

"What happens will happen," she said simply. Long ago, she'd taken those words to heart.

His eyes narrowed. "That's true. Ain't so?"

"God knows what He wants to happen. That's

what we must always remember. *Gott* knows best for us."

"Hey, Ruth?"

"Hmm?"

"Do ya remember your parents?" he asked around a yawn.

Ruth inhaled sharply. No one ever asked about her family. And because the memories hurt too much, she often took care not to think about her parents, too. But the boy was staring at her with so much hope in his eyes, she knew he was thinking about his mother. And about how time moved on.

"I do," she said softly. "My parents were older than most of my friends' parents. I was their surprise baby after fourteen years of marriage. When I came along, they'd long since given up hope of having a family."

"Were they even older than my *daed*?"

She chuckled. "Oh, *jah*. My father was forty-eight when I was born, my *mamm* forty-three."

"What were they like? I mean, besides being so old."

"They were kind, I remember that. And they were kind of goofy."

"Goofy?" His lips curved up. "How did you know?"

"I didn't realize it at the time, I thought all parents were like mine. But after being with other families . . ." Her voice drifted off before she cleared her throat and remembered to keep the pain from her voice. "After being around them, I realized that other mothers and fathers didn't do the things mine did."

"What did your *mamm* and *daed* do?"

"They played games with me. We did things together. Everything was always the three of us," she added, realizing with dismay that she hadn't let herself think of such things in a long time. "Let's see, what else? My *daed* liked to fish. My *mamm* didn't care for it much, but she used to sit with him on the bank and watch. When I came along, I used to sit with them and try to be quiet." As he shifted and yawned again, she smiled. "I'm afraid I never did too good of a job. I liked to talk, you see."

"And then they died?"

"They did." The loss shouldn't hurt so much but it did. She forced herself to continue even though she felt she would rather do just about anything else. "My father had a heart attack and my *mamm* kind of wasted away not long after."

"Did she have a heart attack, too?"

Ruth had always imagined it was more like a broken heart, but that sounded too tragic, too full of angst. So she simply shrugged. "More or less."

"That's sad."

She blinked, struck by the matter-of-fact way he said it. And by the truth of it, too. It was sad. Terribly sad indeed. "It was sad, but it couldn't be helped. The good Lord wanted them up in heaven, you see."

"And now you are okay."

"You are right. Now I am okay." Anxious to move away from the focus on herself, she ruffled his hair. "Just like one day you will be okay, too. These chicken pox will pass, Thomas. I promise."

"I know. Gregory says he's already feeling better."

"See?" She got up. "Now before you get too sleepy, I'm going to draw you a bath."

"Am I allowed to say that I still don't like those baths?"

"Of course you are allowed. But you're still going to have to take one. It will make you feel better."

After drawing the bath and helping Thomas get a fresh towel and clothes to change into, she left him to soak, then checked on the girls again. Since they were still doing all right, she headed downstairs and decided to make some sheets of gingerbread. Tomorrow, perhaps, they could cut out shapes and make some simple houses.

She made the dough, placed it in the oven, then set to make some bean and ham soup.

Soon after she chopped the vegetables, Meg came in to keep her company. Then came the twins. Followed by Gregory and Frank. At last, Katrina joined them.

After filling them all in about their father, she served a simple meal of soup and corn bread and showed them the gingerbread pieces she'd baked.

They'd just finished their simple meals when the back door opened and Martin entered. His cheeks were red from the cold, but he still had a smile for the children.

She washed the children's bowls and plates as he chatted with them and got an update on their spots.

Of course, that led to a flurry of complaints and show-and-tell, each boy or girl anxious to have the worst or best case of chicken pox.

During the next hour, she coaxed the children back to their beds. Meg and Thomas went right to sleep. The others were tucked in and were looking at picture books.

She was just thinking of making herself a cup of hot tea and lying down when she spied Martin sitting by himself at the kitchen table, his bowl of soup practically untouched.

Before she took time to reflect that perhaps he would rather she give him some time and space, she pulled up a chair next to him. "Are you all right?"

Martin lifted his chin and met her gaze. Ruth realized he looked more than a little taken aback, almost as if he was surprised to be asked.

But then he must have seen something in her eyes that reassured him, because he spoke. "I guess I'll have to be all right. Christmas Eve is tomorrow."

He sounded so wistful, he spurred a memory, one she'd long ago hidden away.

Before she could stop herself from revealing something so silly, she murmured, "When I was little, I used to think that the angels were probably busiest on Christmas Eve. I used to go to sleep by imagining them flitting from one place to the next."

He smiled. "That's a nice image. I suppose they are seeing to the needs of their flock—and proclaiming the good news."

Her shoulders relaxed, glad that for whatever reason she'd coaxed a smile from him. "The children will be all right, Martin. None of them are very feverish anymore. Just uncomfortable."

"I'm embarrassed to tell you this, but I've been actually spending most of my time worrying about all those Christmas trees instead of my children." He brushed a hand along his neatly trimmed beard. "I feel guilty about that, but I can't seem to help myself, either. A lot depends on making a profit this month."

"I know. Did everything go okay today?"

He shrugged. "Well enough. It's been better than last year. Not as good as a couple of other years, but *gut*. Plus Floyd said he expects a lot more customers tomorrow morning. That needs to be good enough for me," he said around a sigh. "After all, after tomorrow, the sale will be over. We'll have another season behind us and there won't be much more I can do."

"Much more? Does that mean you'll be open on Christmas Eve?"

He absently brushed a lock of golden brown hair away from his forehead. "We will, but only until one or two."

"I'm surprised that someone would be shopping for trees at such a late date."

"It's usually a pretty busy day. All the trees are deeply discounted, of course. Some folks wait for the sale to put theirs up."

"What do you do with the trees that don't sell?"

"Floyd and a couple of our crew members will take the best ones to a couple of charities early tomorrow. The remaining trees will eventually get made into mulch."

"Nothing will go to waste."

Looking at her in a new way, he shook his head. "You're right. Nothing will go to waste. Nothing of value ever does."

"That's a nice sentiment."

He leaned back, studied her. "Ruth, what happened to you? Why did you always get passed on to a new home?"

Pain slashed through her as she realized that it wasn't just painful memories the question brought; it was also embarrassment.

"I'm not sure what happened. After my mother died, her parents took me in. But they were frail, and after two years, one of my mother's sisters took me in." She winced, remembering her aunt LaVerne and her sons. "But that wasn't a good fit, and so she asked another sibling to watch over me."

She shrugged. "After a while, taking care of me became everyone's Christian duty. And while I am glad for their charity, it was hard to grow up knowing that I was not with them because they wanted me, but because they were obligated."

"I can't imagine what that must have been like."

"I don't want you to have to worry about that. Besides, I survived. Everyone has their own story to tell."

Martin was still gazing at her. It was obvious he was thinking there was more to say, more that he wished to say.

"Really, Martin, it's no different from you. You married a lovely woman, had six perfect *kinner,* and then she passed away. That must have been a terrible loss."

"It was."

She nodded, a little disappointed that he didn't feel compelled to share any more about that. But realizing, too, that there was probably nothing else to say.

Pressing both of his palms on the top of the table, he murmured, "Ruth, Grace was a wonderful woman. She was. She was everything to me. At first the pain was so sharp I swear it hurt to even say her name, to even think it.

"But then, one day, I realized that I had memories of her that were too special to push away. And once I let myself remember our life together, those memories began to bring me a lot of comfort. That's when I realized that those wonderful, crazy, loud children of ours would always be shining examples of Grace's brightness. Of her boldness, too, I guess," he added with a laugh.

"She was bold?"

"Oh, *jah*. She liked to speak her mind, my Grace did. She didn't suffer fools, either." Looking beyond her, Martin smiled. "My Grace? She was something else."

"Ah."

His gaze darted to her again. "But she wasn't perfect, just as I am not. And I also now realize that she's been gone a long time. It's time I made peace with that."

"If you were able to come to terms with her loss, that would be a good thing."

"The Almighty never gives us more than we can handle, does He? Some of the things we must handle are bad. Others worse. But then the next day the sun shines or the snow falls or we get a smile or a hug."

Ruth nodded, realizing that Martin's words were so true. "Those bright mornings and snowy days and warm hugs and sweet smiles make everything else bearable, don't they?"

"*Jah*." Martin nodded. "Sometimes those things make all the difference in the world." Before he walked away he smiled at her.

And Ruth felt that smile deep in her heart.

And she knew he was exactly right.

Chapter 18

Daed said if Jesus got the chicken pox, he wouldn't have complained half as much as me.

Katrina, Age 9

Day 10 of Christmas Break

By ten on the morning of December twenty-fourth, Floyd was all smiles. "We did it, Martin. We sold almost all the trees and were still able to give six beautiful ones to our favorite charities."

Martin shook his head in mock dismay. "I'm starting to think you like giving away those trees as much as selling them."

"I do like giving them away. Makes me feel good to give away something we and the Lord work so hard on." Grinning, he folded his arms over his chest. "I kept out three nine-footers to give to the orphanage.

Those *kinner* are going to have a good time of it, decorating the trees this afternoon."

"I hope so," Martin said softly. He hated the idea of any child being alone in the world. But somehow being alone during the holiday seemed even worse.

"Speaking of children, how goes the chicken pox at your house?"

He grimaced. "They're all in various stages of miserableness. I feel bad for them, I do. But last night I was feeling mighty sorry for myself, too. They're wearing me out." Remembering how tired he'd been last night, and how much Ruth had helped in countless ways, he murmured, "Ruth Stutzman coming to live with us has been a blessing. I wouldn't have been able to function without her."

"And I wouldn't have been able to handle everything here by myself. Looks like we both owe her a lot."

"She said she was going to make a ham and some scalloped potatoes for Christmas. Apple and cherry pies, too. She's making the house feel festive even if there isn't much to celebrate."

"Christmas isn't all about being merry, you know."

"I hear you. But it's also about enjoying special traditions and celebrating being with family and friends. This year, the kids being sick has changed things."

"What did you get Ruth for Christmas?"

Martin glanced at him in surprise. "Nothing."

"What?"

"Why are you surprised?"

"Martin, you better get into town and do something about that."

"You think so? I thought since I was paying her . . ."

"You should do what you want. But personally I would want to have something to give her," he murmured. "It's only right. Ain't so?"

Suddenly he could imagine Christmas morning and the children opening their few presents he'd bought for them. No doubt they would have drawn him pictures.

And Ruth? She would be sitting with them, on the outside looking in again. He couldn't bear to do that to her. "I need to go shopping."

"Go on now."

"Sure? I don't want to leave you with everything."

"I'm sure. Me and Kristy are going to my parents' house tonight and her parents' house tomorrow night, so there isn't much to do. You've got sick kids to fuss over and a special present to buy."

"Right."

Five minutes later, Martin was out the door and hiking down the path to the barn. Once he got there, he paused, knowing the right thing to do would be to go to the house and check in with Ruth and the children. To see if they needed anything.

But he knew that would take at least an hour. It

took time to check in on seven people. And suddenly, he realized that he had things to do.

Christmas had come in spite of everything, and it was time to stop wishing things were different and start looking forward. And there was only one way to do that, by giving something of himself, starting with his heart.

Ruth was using the dining room table as a makeshift laundry station. She'd just brought up a fresh batch of towels, sheets, and dresses from the lines crisscrossing the basement and was carefully folding a pair of pillowcases when she spied Martin leaving the barn in his horse and buggy.

For a moment, she stared after him in shock, surprised that he would be so close yet not stop in at the house to check on the children.

"*Nee*, Ruth," she murmured to herself. "You can pretend for the rest of the world that you are only thinking of the *kinner*, but you know better. You are disappointed that he didn't stop in to check on you."

She frowned as she heard the one word that was still a lie float in her conscious. "All right," she mumbled as she smoothed a towel, then folded it into a neat rectangle. "Not check. You wanted him to visit you. To say hello to you."

Unfortunately, being completely honest didn't make her feel any better.

"That's no fault of his though," she whispered to herself. "That is yours, expecting so much." And that was true.

After placing the last towel neatly on the top of the stack, she picked up a red dress of Meg's and shook out the wrinkles before placing it on a hanger.

For the first time in well, forever, she was allowing herself to feel and hope. She was growing to love the children, and, she realized with a shock of awareness, she was even growing to love Martin.

Last night, when they'd worked on that puzzle by candlelight, she'd never been happier. He'd gazed at her like she was something special.

But more important, she'd felt like she was something special. She felt she was more than just his hired girl, and the children's hired nurse. She'd felt completely wanted.

Looking at the stacks of sheets and towels, at the hangers holding brightly colored little-girl dresses, Ruth realized she'd also allowed herself to want more. For the first time, she was daring to want a family, to want to be seen as someone important.

As someone desirable.

Just as she was about to pick up the towels and return them to the linen closet she noticed a buggy rolling up the drive. When it rolled to a stop in front of the house, she blinked and then blinked again.

Because out of it came three women, and one of them was Lovina Keim.

Unable to stop herself, Ruth grimaced.

Then, of course, she immediately felt bad about that. Looking up at the ceiling, she found herself praying out loud again. "I suppose You have a reason for bringing her here, Lord? Or, perhaps, You are simply showing me that You have an unusual sense of humor. A mighty unusual one at that."

"Ruth, someone's here," Katrina announced as she ran down the stairs.

"Don't run, child. You're going to hurt yourself."

"I won't."

"You mean you haven't yet," she cautioned. "Let's tackle one problem at a time, please," she said just as a knock came at the door.

"Do you know who's here?"

"I do." Remembering that Lovina wasn't exactly the children's favorite person, either, she decided to forgo a warning. Instead, she attempted to smooth the worry from her expression and opened the door wide. "Hello, Lovina. I was folding the laundry in the dining room and saw your buggy."

Lovina looked her over, then peered at Katrina. "Hello, dear."

Katrina grasped Ruth's hand but said nothing.

"Please come in," Ruth said, smiling hesitantly at the two other women. "It's cold outside."

"Ruth, this is my granddaughter, Viola Swartz. And this is Annie. She's a guest in my home, and one of Viola and Ed's missionary friends."

"Pleased to meet you. I'm Ruth. I'm, ah, helping out here for a few days. And this is Katrina."

Lovina glanced at Katrina again, then stilled. "What's wrong with you? You've got something all over your face."

"I have the chicken pox."

"Chicken pox? When did that happen?"

"When Gregory got it."

Viola and Annie giggled at Katrina's comment.

Ruth had to bite back her own temptation to giggle. But not only from Katrina's matter-of-fact answer but Lovina's response, too. Honestly, Lovina was looking at Katrina like she had a strange, deadly virus instead of a common childhood ailment. Then she remembered that not everyone got it at a young age. Warily, she asked, "Have all of you had chicken pox? If not you should probably stay far away from here."

"Bit too late for that. I've had it. And I remember Viola and her twin getting it when they were three or four. What about you, Annie?"

"I've gotten it, too. So we're all safe."

Ruth exhaled. "That's good news. Now, I fear I must let you know that Martin isn't here." She stopped herself just in time from saying that he'd just left in his horse and buggy.

"Oh, we didn't come to see him," Lovina said airily as she slipped off her coat, then reached for Annie's and Viola's cloaks. "We came to see you."

"Me?"

Lovina looked a tad chagrined. "I must admit to feeling a little bit guilty, cajoling you to be here."

"I'm glad you did," Ruth blurted. "I've loved being here." She smiled at Katrina, who was once again staring at her in a worried way. "I've truly enjoyed being around these *kinner*. And Martin, too."

"And Martin, too," Lovina murmured. "Hmm."

Feeling a bit self-conscious, Ruth led them into the kitchen. "I could make some *kaffi*, if you would like some?"

"I would. And once more, I can make it."

"No, I . . . "

"Oh, look!" Annie said, directing everyone's attention to the doorway.

Where the other five kids were staring at Lovina with varying degrees of dread. "You came back," Karin blurted.

"And you should be pleased about that, given that the lot of you look like a litter of Dalmatians," Lovina retorted.

The children scowled.

Annie gasped.

Viola moaned.

But as Ruth gazed at the precious kids, all dressed in flannel nightgowns and pajamas and wearing a whole assortment of mismatched socks on their feet, each one more covered with spots than the last . . . she knew Lovina was right.

They did, kind of look like Dalmatians. And even more, they looked a bit like a pack of puppies, too. They were bunched together, shoulders and arms touching.

She couldn't help it. She started laughing.

Almost as a unit, everyone stared at her in surprise. Then, little by little, the children started giggling. As did Viola.

Annie still looked a little shocked but amused, too.

And Lovina? Lovina Keim, was wearing an expression that could only be described as pleased as punch.

Chapter 19

Christmas is about love and peace and joy. And kittens.

Meg, Age 4

Paying a call on Ruth had been the right thing to do, Lovina decided two hours later when she, Annie, and Viola were packing up to go. Not only had Viola and Annie gotten to meet Ruth, but Lovina felt that they'd also all been able to give Ruth a much-needed break.

And boy, had that poor girl needed a break.

After ascertaining that Ruth was on her own and that the kids were not only itchy and miserable, but also anxious about Christmas, Annie and Viola got right to work.

After Lovina said that she would do some cooking—promising to stay away from anything

to do with liver—the girls took the children upstairs.

Then, in the relative peace of the kitchen, Lovina
sat Ruth down. "Here, dear. Chicken noodle soup."

"*Danke*. It looks *wunderbaar*."

"It's a good batch." Next, she pulled out a box
from the bakery. "Usually, I make fresh rolls, but I
decided to buy two dozen for all of you. Why don't
you have one with some apple butter?"

After inspecting the refrigerator, she decided to
make a shepherd's pie. After setting out a pound of
hamburger, an onion, and a couple of potatoes on
the counter, she went upstairs to see if Viola and
Annie needed any help before she got busy cooking.

But when she peeked into the rooms, it was obvious that the girls had everything well in hand. Lovina
straightened two of the beds, gathered some laundry, then went back downstairs to work on supper.

By this time, Ruth was almost done. When she
saw the laundry, she got to her feet. "Here, let me
help you."

"Nonsense," Lovina said. "I've been doing laundry
for longer than you've been alive."

"But you're a guest—"

"*Nee*, child. I came to help. Please let me. Now,
why don't you go sit for a spell?"

Ruth look tempted, she really did. But on the
edges of her expression was something that seemed

a lot like distrust. Lovina wondered just how many people had let her down in the past.

"Ruth, I promise, I am not doing anything too difficult. Let me help you for a spell. Call it my Christmas gift!"

"But I can't let you do everything."

"Sure you can."

Ruth bit her lip. "But—"

"It's just laundry and supper, dear," Lovina reminded her. "Trust me when I tell you that I've done these things before. Go relax for a little bit."

"Actually, I thought I might go for a little walk, if you don't mind. I haven't left this *haus* for days."

"That's a grand idea." Making a shooing motion with her hands, she murmured, "Take your time. But don't forget to bundle up."

"I'll do that. *Danke.*"

When the back door closed, Lovina smiled to herself and started browning the meat and dicing the onion.

And over the next hour, Viola and Annie were busy as well. They gathered up all the *kinner* to their rooms, organized baths, coated clean children with Calamine lotion, and read stories. Later, they pulled out some construction paper, glue, markers, and scissors, and set them making Christmas cards for their father.

When the shepherd's pie was in the oven, Lovina brought a load of clean laundry upstairs and began putting it all away. It was nice to feel like she was making a difference in others' lives.

And now that she wasn't in charge of the *kinner*, Lovina was finding that she was enjoying being around the Rhodes children very much.

When Brigit had asked if she could make a card for Ruth, too, Annie had given her a hug and said that she thought it was a fine idea. Then, of course, all the children wanted to make special Christmas presents for Ruth, too.

"Mommi, can you keep her busy for a while?" Viola asked.

"Of course, dear."

"Sure?"

Lovina placed her hands on her hips. "You, my dear, have forgotten that most folks are afraid to say 'boo' to me. Convincing Ruth to spend another hour resting or chatting with me won't be difficult at all."

A glint of humor lit Viola's eyes. "Usually I would caution you to not be so heavy-handed. But right now, I think you're just what the *doktah* ordered, Mommi."

Lovina smiled at Viola, Annie, and all the *kinner*

staring up at her with various expressions of doubt and relief.

As she walked back down the stairs, she decided that it had been quite a while since she'd enjoyed an afternoon half so much.

Chapter 20

Frank loves Christmas. And he loves me too.

Gregory, Age 7

Day 11 of Christmas Break

Christmas Day had come.

It was so dark outside, Ruth wasn't sure if it was seven in the morning or seven at night.

Of course, that most likely had to do with her state of mind, she reflected. She'd long passed being tired. Actually, she was pretty sure she'd hit exhausted sometime around noon on Christmas Eve. Right between the time Katrina had burst into tears and Meg had shown off the new blisters that had formed on her calves.

With a feeling of doom, she wrapped a crocheted

afghan around her shoulders and leaned back against the cushions of the couch. Sometime during the last four or five hours she decided to stop using so much energy to walk to her room.

It was much easier to simply close her eyes in the hearth room.

"Ruth?" Martin called out from the kitchen just as the faintest rays of sun were peeking on the horizon. "Did you ever sleep?"

"I slept." And she had, kind of. "Just not in my bed," she said with a smile.

He winced. "I'm sorry about that."

"Don't be. I've been pleased to be of use." Taking a chance, she added, "Actually, I'm mighty glad you've asked me to stay here. It's given me lots to do. And given me a break from my usual routine."

When he entered the room, his eyes looked as bloodshot and tired as she felt. "I wouldn't necessarily call what you've been doing a break. It's been more like an endless amount of work," he murmured. "If I were you I would be trying to run away from here as fast as I could."

Surprised, she looked at him, then smiled softly when she realized he was joking.

So she joked right back. "I've been tempted, but I wouldn't do that to Frank."

"Kind of you."

Looking at the puppy who was now sprawled

asleep on the couch, too worn out from being man-handled by sick children to squirm, Ruth smiled. "I never thought I'd see the day when Frank would be this exhausted."

"That's because most people never get to experience chicken pox times six."

"Praise God for that."

"Amen."

He sat down beside her, propped his feet up on the coffee table.

She said, "I just got out of the boys' room. They're both sound asleep. Gregory looks much better. Thomas looks feverish but he's sleeping."

Continuing the report, she said, "I checked on the twins about three hours ago. They were both itchy and miserable. I rubbed some more lotion on them."

"They're asleep now. And, wonder of wonders, Katrina isn't crying. I don't think she's cried for the last six hours."

"That is *gut* news. *Wunderbaar.*" She wasn't even being sarcastic. For a while last night, Ruth didn't know if she was ever going to be able to get Katrina's tears to stop flowing.

Martin leaned his head back against the couch. "Gosh, here I am, doing it again."

"Doing what?"

"Acting like you have no thoughts except for ones

about my *kinner*." Looking her way, he said, "Merry Christmas, Ruth."

"Don't be so hard on yourself. I have only been thinking about the *kinner*, too. And Merry Christmas to you, too."

And then, she couldn't seem to stop smiling at him. It was like everything she'd been trying so hard to hide needed to shine through.

She was helpless to stop it.

As Martin gazed at her, he felt something warm float over him, and he recognized it for what it was: happiness.

The peaceful kind. The easy kind. The kind that came along when a man was content with his lot in life and his house and home.

He recognized it for what it was, too. A feeling of comfort that he'd once shared with Grace and then, for a while, had convinced himself he'd only imagined.

"I am so sorry that this is how you are having to spend your holidays," he said.

"I thought we were going to stop apologizing to each other."

"That is true, but that was also before things got so bad."

"Please don't take this the wrong way, Martin, but I don't think things are really that bad."

"You actually look like you mean that."

"I do." She rubbed a hand over her eyes in an embarrassed way before she continued. "I'm tired and exhausted and a bit slap-happy. But I'm also happy."

"Truly?" He scanned her face, looking for signs that she was lying.

"Truly. I've spent many Christmases in other people's homes. Most of them, actually. But few families ever made me feel so welcome or so wanted."

"You have been wanted."

"I'm glad I could be of use."

"No, it wasn't your helping hands that made things so special, Ruth. It was your warm heart. It was your smile and your loving nature. It was the way you made each of us feel better just by being you."

"But I didn't do anything." Ruth shook her head like she was trying to shake off the praise.

"You did everything." Though it was tempting to continue to keep his private feelings close to his heart, he knew it was time to be completely open. "You changed this house, made it a home again. You made me realize that things can change for the better. For the first time, I'm not only looking at the past and wishing for things that are no longer there, but I'm thinking about the future. I'm thinking about a future with you."

She blinked. "What are you saying, Martin?"

"I'm saying that I want our relationship to grow and continue to change. I want us to be more than just friends. I want, one day, for you to be mine."

She blinked, her expression a mixture of fear and happiness and cautious hope. And he recognized those emotions because he was feeling the very same ones.

The very same ones.

Grasping her hand, he pressed his lips to her knuckles. "Don't say anything. There's no need. I simply didn't want to go another moment without you knowing how I felt . . . and where I hoped our future would one day be."

Ruth looked at him closely. Opened her mouth. Closed it again.

Then blurted, "I want the same things."

His shoulders eased. His lips curved. He inhaled, preparing to say something more. Say something—anything—to make sure she understood that he had no doubts. . . .

"Snow!" Thomas yelled as he burst into the room.

With a jerk, Martin dropped his hands. "What?"

Ruth got to her feet and walked to the window. Then pressed her hands on the windowsill and her face to the glass. And smiled. "Lots and lots of snow!"

Feet pounded on the floor above them, sounding like a herd of cattle. And then, one by one, each of the *kinner* came flying down the stairs, ignoring Ruth's warnings to walk and to be careful.

But Martin supposed he couldn't blame them.

They'd been spotty and itchy and miserable for days. They'd been missing him and stuck inside.

And now snow had come on Christmas Day.

Meg pulled at his shirt. "Daed! Daddy, snow?"

He scooped her up in his arms and carried her to the window so she could see everything perfectly. "Snow, Meg. A perfect, beautiful, fresh blanket of snow."

"Just for us."

"I think maybe you're right, dear. If there ever was a group of children who deserved a beautiful white Christmas, it would be the six of you."

"And Ruth, too."

"Yes. And Ruth."

Gregory sidled up next to him. "And Frank, too."

"Indeed," Ruth said. "Frank needs some snow, too."

Martin glanced at the line of faces, did a mental head count, then made a decision. Setting Meg back down on the floor, he said, "*Kinner*, hurry and go put on your coats and hats and boots."

"We can go outside even though we're sick?"

"Yep. A little bit of snow on Christmas Day shouldn't hurt anything. We're going outside. We're going to get some fresh air and feel snow on our cheeks. Now, one of you help Meg and go get ready."

With a cheer, they ran through the kitchen and started shuffling against each other to get their items on their bodies.

As the children scattered around them, Ruth met Martin's gaze. Right then and there, time seemed to stop. And just for one small second, they were alone again. Filled with the understanding that this was only the first of many days they were going to have together.

Then, as one of the girls yelled that she couldn't find a mitten, the spell was broken.

Ruth blinked, then started walking toward the line of coats on the wall. "Come on, Martin. It's time, don't you think? It's time to enjoy the first snowfall of the season. It's always the best, don't you think?"

"I do," he said as he opened the back door wide and stepped outside, Frank barking at his heels.

Chapter 21

*Our snow angels are pretty. The prettiest angels
ever.*

Karin, Age 5

The snow had begun falling sometime in the middle
of the night. Early that morning, soon after Lovina
prepared her butternut squash casserole, she walked
out onto the big front porch and watched the snow
continue to fall. Each flake was big and fluffy, perfectly beautiful. The kind of snow meant for children to play in.

Behind her, the door opened. "Lovina, you're
going to catch your death. Come in from the cold."

Because she was feeling a little chilled, she immediately complied. Once inside, she picked up her
warm mug of coffee again. "It's Christmas, Aaron."

"It is, at that. Merry Christmas."

She smiled back at him. "Merry Christmas to you, too."

"Do you think we'll all still be able to get to Elsie's *haus* today?"

"Of course." Suddenly, he grinned in a way he hadn't in years, making him look almost boyish. "I betcha Peter's already gotten out the sleigh."

"Aaron, when was the last time we went for a sleigh ride? Five years ago?"

"More like ten." Moving closer, he said, "I seem to remember thinking that we were too old for sleigh rides." He shook his head. "Now I realize that was a foolish thought. I'm finding myself eager to glide through the fields for a bit."

Lovina chuckled. "Me, too." Thinking about how fun it was going to be to sit with her family while the horses trotted, the bells on their harnesses ringing merrily, she sighed. "It's going to be a *wonderful-gut* day. And guess what? All I had to make was some squash."

Aaron placed an arm around her shoulder. "We can enjoy the day while our granddaughters fret and fuss. What do you think, dear? Will they be up to the task of feeding all of us Keims?"

"Of course. But it doesn't matter if everything isn't perfect. Not really. Because we're going to have lots of our family together. That's a blessing."

Her husband's eyes softened. "It is that. We are blessed beyond words to still be alive on this earth.

To have each other. To have our *kinner* and our grandchildren."

"And our great-grandchildren."

"Blessed beyond measure," he murmured. "I'm going to go to the barn to check on the horses."

"Peter and Roman will take care of the horses."

"No, I don't think so," he retorted. "It's Christmas morning. I have a need to walk around for a bit." His lips curved. "And, of course, see if the animals are talking."

Remembering that old story, she chuckled. "The animals talk to each other on Christmas Eve, not Christmas morning."

"Just to be on the safe side, I'll go do some checking."

After he left, she tightened her robe a bit more securely, slipped her feet into her cozy slippers, and padded into the kitchen, just in time to see Annie come out of the spare bedroom. "Merry Christmas, Annie!"

"Merry Christmas." Annie's eyes bright with happiness, she said, "Did you know it's snowing?"

"I did. And because of the snow, we'll all be going to Elsie's *haus* in a sleigh."

"I can't wait," Annie said as she helped herself to a cup of coffee.

Lovina smiled at her, then noticed that Annie didn't seem completely happy. "Annie, you look a little blue. Are you all right?"

She shrugged. "I was merely wishing that my visit here wasn't almost over."

"You've enjoyed your time here in Ohio, haven't you?"

"I have. I really have." Her brown eyes were shining. Lovina wasn't sure if it was disappointment or if she was on the verge of tears.

All Lovina did know was that she felt the same way.

"What . . . What would you think about staying here?"

Annie's chin popped up. "What do you mean?"

"I mean that Aaron and I would love to have you stay with us even after Viola and Edward go back to Belize. If that is something you might like, that is."

"You really wouldn't mind my staying?"

Lovina shook her head. "I wouldn't mind at all. In fact, I would love your company."

"But what would I do?"

Lovina shrugged. "You could do what the rest of us do, dear. Spend time with friends. Visit Elsie and those Rhodes *kinner*. Plant a garden, make a quilt, read books, go for walks. Learn to bake." She winked. "Who knows? Maybe even fall in love one day."

"Do you think I really could stay?"

"Annie, dear. I've learned that with God all things are possible. If you want to do this, all you have to do is let me know. We'll talk to Viola and Edward and then we'll call your father, too."

Annie stared at her for a long moment before nodding. "*Danke*, Lovina. I would like that. I mean . . . I would love that very much."

"It's settled, then. Now, you'd best get yourself ready to spend the day at Elsie's!"

After giving her a quick, exuberant hug, Annie darted out of the kitchen.

Feeling happy and excited about Annie's decision, Lovina poured herself another cup of coffee, then decided to take it back to the big easy chair in their bedroom. Though the day was sure to be busy, there was time to watch the snow some more.

And as she did, she thought about how it covered everything up. But only temporarily.

And thought about how that was Christ's rebirth.

And how the Lord brought them snow at all the most important points in their lives. When things needed to be covered up and briefly forgotten, snow came, making all the ugly in life beautiful for a short time.

Making everything perfect and fresh. New.

Then, of course, He would ensure that nothing covered up would last long. It would be briefly out of mind and out of sight . . . until the weather warmed or the sun came out.

Much of it like the rhythm of their lives and her family. For a brief time their bonds had been covered up, lost in the grime of daily living.

Or maybe it was their faith that had needed to be cleansed. Now time had come full circle. The Lord was giving them another opportunity to make things fresh and new in their family. Forcing them to stay together for just a little while longer.

That first snowfall of the season was everything.

It was unexpected and exciting and nerve-wracking and beautiful. It was cold and icy and dangerous and perfect.

It was like faith. And love. Like everything worth remembering. Like everything that was special and meaningful.

Like Christmas Day.

Epilogue

Everything happens for a reason. We know that now.

Thomas, Age 8

Night had come, and with it the six Rhodes children at last fell into an exhausted slumber. Ruth was only surprised they'd stayed awake so long.

It had been an eventful day, for sure and for certain. After Martin had opened the door and the children had run out into the yard like they'd been prisoners getting an hour's reprieve, the eight of them built snowmen and made snow angels and threw snowballs and generally wore themselves out.

To be honest, there was a part of Ruth that worried the whole time about letting such sick *kinner* do so much. But she'd also lived long enough to recognize the importance of grasping everything good when it was possible.

After almost a full hour, the eight of them had trudged back in, the children had changed into fresh pajamas, and she had served them all a breakfast of blueberry French toast, crisp bacon, and mugs and mugs of creamy hot chocolate.

And by this time, for sure . . . the children had been thinking about presents.

She'd given each of them her gift—slippers and stuffed animals that she'd bought over a week ago. She'd also presented each of them with a mason jar with their name carefully painted on the side. At the top of each jar, she'd used one of Martin's tools and made a small opening, big enough for a quarter. And inside each, she'd put in four quarters.

Martin gave them some trains and a plastic farm-animal set, as well as each of them a book and a new pair of cozy pajamas. And then, with a very big smile, he led a bundled-up Meg to the barn and returned fifteen minutes later with a very happy Meg and one mewing calico kitten.

The kids gave him their pictures and cards.

And for the first time, Ruth didn't care that she was merely a visitor in another family's home. Because she felt like she was a part of them. She felt their love for one another, and their love for her.

And even more, she realized that she and Martin did have a future together. He cared about her, just as she cared about him. Here, in this house full of noise and laughter and tears and hugs, she'd found love. She knew that one day she would be the children's new mother and Martin's wife.

But then, to her great surprise, she found herself surrounded by all six *kinner*, each holding a card just for her. And Martin, holding a beautifully wrapped box.

"I didn't expect this."

Martin smiled. "That's why giving you things is so much fun, Ruth."

Each card was adorable. Meg drew a heart, the twins drew pictures of everyone together, each child looking like a spotted Dalmatian.

Gregory had divided his picture into fourths and had drawn four different pictures of Frank. Thomas had drawn a simple Christmas tree. And Katrina? She had drawn a picture of a sleigh in the snow with lots of presents inside and a lady, too—Ruth.

Ruth hugged the pictures to her chest. "These are the best gifts I've ever gotten," she said, trying her best to hold off tears.

"Here's one more," Martin said quietly. "I didn't make it, but I hope you will like it, too."

To her embarrassment, her hands shook as she carefully unwrapped the gift, then opened the lid.

But then, she couldn't do anything but gasp as she pulled out the most remarkable snow globe she'd ever seen.

"Do you like it?" he whispered.

"It's *wunderbaar.* Absolutely wonderful," she said around a gasp. "It's perfect."

His face relaxed into a smile. "I was going to give it to you as a reminder that snow always does come. Maybe not when we hope for it, maybe it takes too long. But always here, when the snow does fall, it's the perfect time."

"Just like today," Katrina said.

"*Jah,*" Ruth said as she gazed at the children and then looked up at Martin. "It does come at the right time. And when it does, it's clean and fresh and good. Just like today."

"You mean, just like today, Christmas Day," Brigit corrected.

Ruth leaned back and laughed. "*Jah,* dear. Just like today. Today, our wonderful, so, so special Christmas Day."

About the author

About the book

Insights,
Interviews
& More...

Read on

Meet
Shelley Shepard Gray

The New Studio

PEOPLE OFTEN ASK how I started writing. Some believe I've been a writer all my life; others ask if I've always felt I had a story I needed to tell. I'm afraid my reasons couldn't be more different. See, I started writing one day because I didn't have anything to read.

I've always loved to read. I was the girl in the back of the classroom with her nose in a book, the mom who kept a couple of novels in her car to read during soccer practice, the person who made weekly visits to the bookstore and the library.

Back when I taught elementary school, I used to read during my lunch breaks. One day, when

I realized I'd forgotten to bring something to read, I turned on my computer and took a leap of faith. Feeling a little like I was doing something wrong, I typed those first words: *Chapter One*.

I didn't start writing with the intention of publishing a book. Actually, I just wrote for myself.

For the most part, I still write for myself, which is why, I think, I'm able to write so much. I write books that I'd like to read. Books that I would have liked to have in my old teacher tote bag. I'm always relieved and surprised and so happy when other people want to read my books, too!

Another question I'm often asked is why I choose to write inspirational fiction. Maybe at first glance, it does seem surprising. I'm not the type of person who usually talks about my faith in the line at the grocery store or when I'm out to lunch with friends. For me, my faith has always felt like more of a private thing. I feel that I'm still on my faith journey—still learning and studying God's word.

And that, I think, is why writing inspirational fiction is such a good fit for me. I enjoy writing about characters who happen to be in the middle of their faith journeys, too. They're not perfect, and they don't always make the right decisions. Sometimes they make mistakes, and sometimes they do something they're proud of. They're characters who are a lot like me.

Only God knows what else He has in store for me. He's given me the will and the ability to write stories to glorify Him. He's put many people in my life who are supportive and caring. I feel blessed and thankful . . . and excited to see what will happen next! ᗡ

Letter from the Author

Dear Reader,

Thank you for picking up *Snowfall*. I dearly love to write Christmas books, and I particularly enjoyed writing this one, my bow to one of my favorite musicals ever, *The Sound of Music*. Those Rhodes children made me laugh. Maybe it's because I taught elementary school for years, but I've always had a soft spot for children in books who are a little squirrely.

One day while I was writing this novella, I was thinking about Ruth and Christmas and all those kids . . . and I knew I needed to heap on the problems. I started thinking about the years when my two kids were little and when I felt especially overwhelmed. And that's when I remembered their having the chicken pox.

Now, I guess, kids get immunized for the chicken pox. Of course that's a good thing. But a part of me is going to feel just a little bit sorry for those parents who aren't going to have their own chicken pox battle stories to share. It seemed like a rite of passage, just like those terrible twos or when teenagers get their driving permits.

I remember my children having the chicken pox better than they do, mainly because they were very small. My daughter was three months old, my son twenty-one months old. They got the chicken pox right after my daughter had been in the hospital for croup and my son had had the stomach flu. I remember all this because I was teaching fourth grade, my husband had just started a new job, and we had to alternate taking days off work. I don't think I'll ever be that tired again!

Of course, the kids got through it just fine. Their parents did, too. All we have to remember of that week are a couple of scars and some photos.

Oh, and the memories! Nothing brought my husband and me closer than taking care of sick kids. As soon as I started writing those scenes with Martin and Ruth taking care of all those kids, I knew my hero and heroine were going to be just fine. If they could survive the chicken pox at Christmas, they could survive just about anything!

I hope you, on the other hand, have been enjoying a worry-free and stress-free holiday! I hope you're planning to celebrate Christ's birth with family and friends and cookies and a turkey or two.

But if, by chance, things aren't perfect, I hope you will find God's blessings in the littlest of things, too. A good book, a warm fire, or, perhaps, a really beautiful snowfall.

> Wishing you many blessings,
> and a Merry Christmas, too!
> Shelley Shepard Gray

Questions for Discussion

1. Did you have a favorite character in *Snowfall*? I have to admit that I was very fond of Ruth, mainly because she was so competent! That is not like me at all. I would have been much more like Lovina when faced with the possibility of babysitting six children! Who do you know that could have handled such a job with ease? Why?

2. I have a feeling that a lot of us grow up hearing that it is better to give than to receive. Is that true with you? What do you especially enjoy giving? Your time, your talents, the perfect gift?

3. I loved the idea of making Ruth once again a visitor in a home at Christmas. Why do you think she finally felt like she was a part of the family? Was it her love for Martin or something else?

4. It was important for me to let readers who were familiar with my book *Eventide* see how Elsie is doing. What did you think about her desire to be in charge of the dinner? Why do you think she felt the need to take this on in the first place?

5. I really thought Lovina needed Annie in her life. Where do you see their relationship heading?

6. So, do you have a chicken pox story of your own? What do you or your children remember most about this illness?

7. What did you think about Martin? Did you think Ruth was a good match for him? Why or why not?

8. I must admit that I wrote most of this novella during the coldest, snowiest winter I could ever remember! It was sometimes hard to make my characters yearn for snow! Have you ever experienced a white Christmas? What are some of your family's favorite winter traditions? ∾

A Sneak Peek of Shelley Shepard Gray's Next Book, *A Promise at Palm Grove*

Keep reading for a sneak peek from the first book in Shelley's upcoming Amish Brides of Pinecraft series!

A PROMISE AT PALM GROVE

The story of a bride-to-be torn between the man she's agreed to wed—and the man her heart desires.
Coming Spring 2015 from Avon Inspire.

"COME ON, GIRLS."

Mattie froze. "Why?"

"To see the boys, of course."

Leona shook her head. "Sara, we can't simply go search for those boys."

"You can't. You're engaged. But I can," she called over her shoulder. "Come on." And with that, she darted down Burky Street and turned left on Beneva Road.

After exchanging a pained look with Mattie, Leona hustled down the sidewalk after Sara. There was no way she was going to let Sara get in trouble on her own.

After practically running down the block, Sara came to a sudden stop at the front yard of the Palm Grove Mennonite Church.

"Now what's wrong?" Mattie griped before she, too, seemed transfixed by the sight before her.

Feeling like the lazy part of the Three Musketeers, Leona hurried over to catch up, then found herself staring at the sight, too.

And then she had to remind herself not to stare quite so blatantly.

But what a sight it was!

"What are they doing?"

"It looks like there's something in the tree."

Two men about their age had surrounded a

tree and had their chins lifted, and were staring at something nestled in the branches. Leona followed their gazes, then stifled a gasp.

A third man was more or less reclining on one of the branches like he was seven years old again. One leg was swinging, his blue shirt was untucked, and his straw hat had floated down to the base of the tree. And he was grinning like he was having the best time in the world.

Leona swallowed.

Yes, it was obvious that they were having a good time. Every minute or two they laughed and egged each other on and made jokes about bees.

Bees!

Especially the man in the tree, who she just happened to notice had sandy-brown hair, very tan arms, and a dimple.

She knew he had a dimple because from the moment she'd spied him he'd been either laughing, teasing his buddies, or grinning.

He lit up the scene. And, she had a feeling, most likely lit up wherever he was all the time. Unable to take her eyes off him, she realized he was the type of man she used to dream about when she went to sleep at night.

He looked confident and happy. Comfortable with himself and with everyone else, too.

Just then, that man glanced in her direction. Within seconds his gaze became intent. Far more serious.

And though it was truly a fanciful thought, Sara imagined that she could actually feel his gaze. And that he was thinking the same thing she was—that for the first time in forever, he was seeing something important.

That look was compelling and scary and intense. Enough to take her breath away. Instinctively, she took a step back. "We should go."

"No way," Sara said. And then did the exact opposite. She walked a little bit closer. "I want to see what they're doing."

"But it's none of our business."

"We won't get in the way, Leona," Mattie said. "Don't be so timid. I mean, weren't you saying on the bus that you wanted to meet new people?"

She had said that. But she hadn't been talking about handsome men. She'd been thinking more along the lines of girls their own age. "Yes, but—"

"But nothing," Sara whispered. "They're cute and they look nice. And they're Amish, so even my *mamm* wouldn't get mad."

At that Leona felt her lips twitch. Sara's mother constantly warned Sara about talking to Englischers, especially young, handsome Englischers. "Fine."

"Hey!" one of the guys called out.

"Hey, yourself," Sara said, flirting right back.

"Did you need something?"

"*Nee*. We were just wondering what caught your attention. What's in the tree?"

"A cat. A mighty determined, mighty skittish *kats*."

Mattie laughed. "I guess it takes three Amish men to rescue a cat in Pinecraft?" ▶

A Sneak Peek of Shelley Shepard Gray's
Next Book, *A Promise at Palm Grove*
(continued)

The man's smile grew wider. "Obviously, and we're still having a time of it. Perhaps you three ought to come over here and give us a hand."

Before any of the girls could comment on that, there was a rustle of leaves followed by a lazy, loud *meow*. Then, next thing they knew, a sleek gray cat with white paws gracefully leaped from the tree like it was the headline attraction in a carnival show.

"She's out! Catch her!" the man in the tree called as he started his descent.

The blond who had been flirting with Sara reached for the cat, missed, and stumbled as he attempted to regain his balance and run after the wayward cat at the same time.

In response, the cat meowed, lifted her chin, then darted toward the girls.

"Oh!" Sara said. "She's pretty."

"She is mighty pretty," Leona agreed as the cat pranced to her legs, circled around her ankles, then looked up at Leona with her gray-blue eyes and meowed.

Before she thought about it, Leona bent down and picked it up.

"*Meow,*" the cat uttered again before snuggling close, purring her contentment. Hugging it close to her, Leona gazed helplessly at her cousins and at the three men who had now all turned to her with looks of wonder.

And then the man from the tree branches stepped forward and grinned. "Perhaps it doesn't take three Amish men at all. Just one pretty blond girl."

Leona knew he was teasing.

She knew he was being a mite too forward.

She knew she was engaged and shouldn't encourage any familiarity.

But for some reason, all she could do was stare at him, cuddle the cat.

And smile right back. ᐧᐧ